HALFHYDE
GOES TO WAR

D1614276

HALFHYDE GOES TO WAR

PHILIP McCUTCHAN

St. Martin's Press
New York

Library of Congress Cataloging-in-Publication Data

McCutchan, Philip, 1920–
    Halfhyde goes to war.

    1. South African War, 1899–1902—Fiction.
2. Great Britain—History, Naval—Fiction.
I. Title.
PR6063.A167H315   1987   823'.914   87-4360
ISBN 0-312-00603-9

First published in Great Britain by George Weidenfeld & Nicolson Limited.

First U.S. Edition

10 9 8 7 6 5 4 3 2 1

HALFHYDE
GOES TO WAR

ONE

'It's not fair,' Victoria said. She stamped her foot. 'It's not bloody fair, mate! Didn't you tell them that?'

'No,' Halfhyde answered evenly.

'Oh, for God's sake. Why ever *not*?'

'Because it was scarcely the argument to advance to a post captain in Her Majesty's fleet, Victoria – especially at a time when the country's at war and –'

'With a bloody load of Boer farmers –'

'And we are in Cape Town and I happen to hold a lieutenant's commission in the reserve. And kindly don't shout at me in public, Victoria. I refuse to appear hen-pecked in front of troops and Kaffirs. We shall go back aboard. Then you may rant in privacy.'

'Rant, eh!' The small pixie face was crumpled; she was close to tears. Urchin-like, she moved a few paces ahead of Halfhyde, then turned back and took his arm. 'Sorry, mate. Maybe I do rant.'

'You do indeed. Had you not done so, I wouldn't have said you did. I am a man of my word, Victoria.'

'Oh, the great I Am. Look, you don't love me, do you?'

'Yes,' Halfhyde snapped.

'I don't –'

'We won't go into that again,' Halfhyde said.

He strode on beneath the hot sun, tall, cadaverous, making for the *Glen Halladale* alongside the wall in the docks, a shipmaster with a deal of worry on his mind, not the least of his worries being Victoria Penn, brought – not by any act of his own – from Sydney to Liverpool and thence, after one of the most hazardous voyages Halfhyde had ever undertaken, here to Cape Town. Victoria had grown upon him; he was fond of her and felt responsible for her. For her part, he knew, he virtually ranked with God. She had expected to sail the seas aboard his ship, the master's unofficial mate to the end of time, right into the last sunset.

But Captain Gorleston Wemyss-Buchanan, Royal Navy, Chief of Staff to the Admiral commanding at the Cape, had had other ideas.

ii

The port was crammed with shipping of all sorts, troopships from India and the Mediterranean, passenger liners converted into hired transports, cargo vessels, colliers, store ships to supply the military. Both steam and sail were represented; the *Glen Halladale* was not the only full-rigged ship at the berths. And the town swarmed with troops in khaki from Great Britain and the Empire. It seemed to Halfhyde that half the world's armies had come to the aid of the old Queen in Windsor Castle: Queensland Mounted Infantry in their bush hats, Imperial Light Horse, Royal Canadian Artillery, New Zealand roughriders, gunners from Sierra Leone, Lumsden's Horse from Assam as well as any number of regiments from home – Royal Dublin Fusiliers, Connaught Rangers, Gloucesters, Border Regiment, Duke of Cornwall's Light Infantry, Lancers, Hussars, gunners, sappers, medical detachments . . . it was quite a lot, Halfhyde thought, to deal with disorganized Boer levies. But in all truth the war had not been going very well for the imperial forces. There had been a retreat upon the township of Ladysmith, now under siege by the Boers along with Kimberley and Mafeking.

Halfhyde, on his arrival in Simon's Town from Devonport in the *Glen Halladale*, had felt aloof from the war activity; this was to be a land campaign and no concern for seamen, although there were a number of warships in Table Bay. Once he had landed the draft of convicts from Dartmoor Prison and had been given an official receipt for them by the military authorities, who were taking them, volunteers all, into army service as pioneers, and once he had shifted berth to the docks in Table Bay and discharged the gold bullion, Halfhyde had believed he had only to await orders for his next voyage. These orders might be for the Channel and a home port or they might be for anywhere as required by the authorities, for the *Glen Halladale* was under government charter.

Victoria had been looking forward to the delights of Cape Town. The outward voyage had not been easy for her. Now was the time for enjoyment of a new land. The war was a long way north; it need not impact.

'Just look at that,' she'd said as they had come in sight of Table Mountain, flat as a pancake at its summit with a mist lying over it, a pinkish-white mist. 'Bloody marvellous! Beats Sydney, I reckon.'

They had gone ashore that night, together with Edwards, Halfhyde's first mate, for a celebratory dinner at a smart hotel. Halfhyde and Edwards had celebrated a safe arrival rather too well; it had been Victoria's task to see them back aboard, and much ribald song had issued from the horse-drawn cab that had taken them back to the docks. In the morning, Halfhyde's hangover had not been helped by her recriminations.

'Bloody pissed again. Do all seamen always get bloody drunk in port?'

'Yes.' Halfhyde spoke through clenched teeth.

'Bloody disgusting, I call it.'

'Go ashore and find a soldier.'

She said loudly, 'I've a bloody good mind to – except that I reckon they get drunk too.'

'So do I.'

'For God's sake. Men!'

'You should have got used to them in Australia.'

Halfhyde struggled into his clothes. The tea brought by his steward had at least dampened the bird-cage dryness of his mouth and tongue but he felt fiendishly ill. Victoria's mop of fair hair smote his eyes as a ray of strong sunlight through the cabin port seemed to turn it to shining gold. That morning he ate no breakfast in the saloon; no more did Edwards. Victoria Penn, grinning all over her face, ate three breakfasts. Halfhyde and Edwards stamped out on deck, leaving her to them.

Halfhyde looked up at his bare masts, at the work proceeding on deck under the bosun as everything was washed down, the scene of activity lit by a sparkling sun and a clear blue day. It was early yet; the air was invigorating before the day's full heat set in. Halfhyde was inspecting the holds from which the filth of the convict draft had almost all been cleaned away when a bluejacket messenger came up the brow from the dockside. The naval rating approached the bosun and was directed to wait. The bosun called down to the hold, and Halfhyde came up. He raised an eyebrow at the messenger.

'Captain Halfhyde, sir?'

Halfhyde nodded.

'A letter, sir. From the Admiral's office.'

Halfhyde took the envelope with the Admiralty crest on the back, broke the seal and tore it open. He read swiftly. The letter was from the Chief of Staff.

'Damnation!' He was, it seemed, required to wait upon Captain Wemyss-Buchanan at the Admiral's office. To the messenger he said, 'The damnation is between you and me. You may tell Captain Wemyss-Buchanan's secretary that I shall be with the Chief of Staff at noon.'

iii

The orders required him to attend in his uniform as a lieutenant of the Royal Naval Reserve. As he pulled on the monkey-jacket with the two gold stripes of interwoven braid he reflected that this was significant. Something was in the wind. Victoria sensed it too; she was uneasy, her face had lost its brightness.

Halfhyde took her ashore with him, since if he had not done so the song and dance might well have been heard over the whole of Cape Town. Halfhyde, a leader of men and a man of much authority aboard his ship, wondered why it was that he

4

was so inept when it came to women – to Victoria at all events. It was simply not in him to be too harsh with her except when she came between him and his duty to his command. This was not one of those occasions; it was no concern of Captain Wemyss-Buchanan whether or not he was accompanied by a woman, though he would not take her to the Chief of Staff's office. He arranged to meet her at a hotel at 1.30 p.m., but not the one where they'd dined; Victoria refused to show her face there again after last night.

She said, 'Don't be late, eh?'

'I've a feeling that will scarcely be up to me. But I shall do my best.'

'Just tell him, mate. You're captain of your own ship, aren't you?'

Halfhyde sighed; Victoria Penn knew nothing of the ways of Her Majesty's fleet and its sometimes costive senior officers, men of much self-importance and not to be argued with nor hurried in one's own interest. But as it happened the interview with the Chief of Staff was both prompt and reasonably brief.

Captain Gorleston Wemyss-Buchanan was a taciturn man, as tall and thin as Halfhyde himself, and one with a nervous twitch that caused him never to be still but to pace up and down whilst talking and every now and again to reach behind himself and give a hitch to the seat of his trousers. He had the air of wanting to get all business over and done with in the shortest possible time. Possibly he was a busy man; at any rate, he said he was.

'Day's always too short, Halfhyde. Sit down.'

Halfhyde sat; Wemyss-Buchanan paced back and forth, casting a long shadow on the wall opposite his window. 'War's not going too well. General Buller has asked for more guns. Asked for a naval brigade in fact. Well?'

'I beg your pardon, sir?'

'How's your gunnery? As a reserve officer it'll not be up to much – you people are seamen, not gunners. But I happen to know you were a regular officer until a couple of years ago – a lieutenant RN.'

'True, sir.' True it was: disagreements over the years with addle-minded admirals had led to Halfhyde leaving the navy to conduct his life more independently as an owner-master in the merchant service. It had been on account of the unusual nature of the voyage just ended that he had been given a reserve commission; he had not really expected that he would be called upon to serve.

He said, 'I was never a gunnery specialist, sir. I was a salt horse.'

'But you'll know enough. Your early training, you see.'

'Yes.'

'Good!' Wemyss-Buchanan appeared relieved. 'Officers can't be spared from the warships in port, Halfhyde. Not at this moment – more ships will arrive shortly but General Buller's request is urgent. An armoured train leaves Cape Town for Chieveley railway station tomorrow at 6 a.m. With it will go a battery of three 4.7 guns with naval crews.'

'And me, sir?'

'Yes, Halfhyde.' Wemyss-Buchanan pulled at the slack of his trouser-seat. 'And there's something else.'

The 'something else' was the gold bullion discharged from the *Glen Halladale*'s double bottoms where it had voyaged from Devonport beneath the hold that had been turned into convict accommodation: that gold had had a shady origin, an unauthorized, clandestine cargo intended as a means of ensuring co-operation from Halfhyde in the attempted unlawful extraction of one of the convicts whilst on passage and the man's transference to what had been virtually a pirate vessel, a privately-owned steam yacht that had overtaken the *Glen Halladale*. All this had since been regularized and there had been no trouble accruing to Halfhyde. But now, it seemed, there was a use for the gold, which amounted in value to something over a hundred thousand pounds sterling. And that gold bullion was to be the real reason for Halfhyde's presence aboard the armoured train for Chieveley.

iv

It had been when he met Victoria at the hotel as arranged that the girl had burst out that it wasn't fair. Halfhyde was not even giving her lunch ashore: he would be too busy, he said, and must return aboard as soon as possible.

'Where's this bloody Chieveley?'

'Outside Ladysmith.'

She stared in dismay. 'You're not bloody going there!'

'I am indeed, Victoria –'

'You bloody can't!'

He frowned. 'Try to remember this isn't Sydney.'

'Eh?'

'The constant use of the word "bloody", Victoria. They may not like it in South Africa for all I know – from a lady.'

'I'm bloody not a lady, mate. And it's a dinkum Aussie word.'

'And thus best left in Australia. Outside Australia it can grow monotonous.'

'Oh, all *right*,' she said. 'I'll bloody try.' She added rather dismally, 'But don't expect too much, eh?' She walked on in silence for a while, then asked, 'What about me? I don't count, I s'pose?'

'Not to Captain Wemyss-Buchanan.'

'Huh!' She was scornful. 'Bloke with a name like that, he'd not last long down under.'

'Never mind that, Victoria. To answer your question, you'll remain aboard my ship. The *Glen Halladale* will leave for Durban tomorrow, under Edwards' command, and it's in Durban that I shall pick her up again.'

'When?'

'In due course.'

'Don't give much away, do you?'

He shrugged; he said nothing about the bullion. They returned aboard, neither saying much. Victoria was holding back tears: a voyage around the Cape of Good Hope to Durban in Natal would be no fun without St Vincent Halfhyde, and in time of war anything might happen to him and she might never see him again; she would be alone and friendless in a land at war and might be forced back into the old ways, the ways that she believed she'd left behind her when Halfhyde had come into her life in Sydney – so long ago now it seemed. She'd had to make a living; there was always something a woman had to sell, and she couldn't afford to be fussy. A hopeless future drifted across her mind, haunting her.

For his part, Halfhyde was much preoccupied. The command of a naval gun-battery of itself held no fears, except that of possibly appearing out-of-date in front of his gunner's mate, who would be a petty officer of experience and long training in the complexities of modern gunnery; nor did war itself hold any fears. When he had first entered the navy via the old training-ship *Britannia* he had met head-on the concept of the ultimate object of a naval officer's career: war. Those who served Queen Victoria went with the prospect of death at their elbow, and the sea itself was also a hard taskmistress. But the gold bullion was different. Surrounded with chicanery from the time it had come aboard, surrounded with the threat of death, it had about it a dirty feel.

Orders as to its final destination would reach him later. Wemyss-Buchanan had already told him that the gold would be moved from a military strong-room to the armoured train at 4 a.m. next day, with an escort of military policemen and accompanied by a Mr Bewdley from the Cape secretariat.

That afternoon Halfhyde went in naval transport to the dockyard at Simon's Town, where he boarded the heavy cruiser *Terrible* to assist in the operation of disembarking what was to be his 4.7 battery to the dockside, lowering the guns into carriages that would take them to the railway station in Cape Town. With them would go thirty-three seamen gunners plus three leading seamen and a gunner's mate. The latter was a hard-looking, bearded petty officer second class named Dunning, a man with the look of a strict driver of men and a tongue that lashed like a whip. There would be no slackness while Dunning was around, so much was obvious. Halfhyde took the bull by the horns.

'I'm a seaman, Petty Officer Dunning. I have the rudiments of gunnery and no more. I shall look to you to improve my knowledge.'

'You'll not look in vain, sir.'

'Good! I trust we shall make a useful team.' Halfhyde spoke to some extent tongue-in-cheek: he didn't expect his connection with the battery to last for long. The bullion loomed and nagged. Perhaps Mr Bewdley would be able to cast some light.

v

From the *Terrible* Halfhyde made his way into Cape Town and sought the services of a solicitor. His mission sounded dangerous to say the least – potentially so at any rate, in the absence of specific information as to the bullion's destination and use – and he had Victoria Penn to think of. The *Taronga Park* back in Liverpool, or wherever the ship might now be on government requisition, still remained his own property and would one day, when the war was over and he had relinquished his reserve commission, be returned to him by the British Admiralty. The *Taronga Park* it was that had brought Victoria Penn with him across the world from Sydney to Liverpool. The ship had loomed large in her life and if he should die he wished it to become hers. In the absence of a will the ship would go to his estranged but still legal wife, the terrible Mildred, now – and, Halfhyde hoped, for ever more – with her parents in Portsmouth, happy enough with the horses she maintained upon a farm in Hampshire, and her attendance at every meeting possible in the racing calendar and untroubled by her absent husband's natural desires for her body, advances that she had rejected from the first night of the long-ago honeymoon . . . .

Early next morning Halfhyde held Victoria in his arms and told her of the making of a will; he wished only to reassure her as to her future. She was sleepy, almost drugged with tiredness; there hadn't been much sleep during their last night together. She looked at the clock on the bulkhead as Halfhyde got up and lit the lantern hanging in gimbals from the cabin's deckhead.

'For God's sake,' she said. 'It's only bloody three in the bloody morning . . . .'

'Yes. Did you hear what I said, Victoria?'

'Eh?'

'I've made a will.' He said it all over again.

She burst into tears, got out of the bunk and clung to him.

'Don't go, mate! Don't bloody go, *please*!'

Gently he lifted her away. She was unable to stop crying. Soon Halfhyde heard the sound of transport, hooves and iron-rimmed wheels clattering on the dockside stone. By the time his steward had come aft to report the carriage alongside he was dressed and ready, wearing a khaki-drill uniform provided by one of the *Terrible*'s officers and now adorned with his own RNR shoulder-straps. Victoria went to the gangway with him, her face a desolate mess and her hair, as usual, awry. Edwards was at the gangway to bid the Captain god-speed. Halfhyde shook the first mate's hand.

'I trust my absence will not be a long one, Mr Edwards. Meanwhile I leave the ship in good hands. And you'll have a care for Miss Penn.'

'I will that, sir.'

Halfhyde nodded and moved for the head of the gangway. They were not the only ones awake at an ungodly hour: a melancholy voice came from the fo'c'sle-head, raised in song:

> 'And fare thee weel, my only love!
> And fare thee weel a while!
> And I will come again, my love,
> Though it were ten thousand mile.'

Halfhyde glanced at Victoria's face in the light from the gangway lantern. He could have murdered the singer. The oaf had made Victoria much worse.

TWO

The railway station was a cold and gloomy place; the armoured train, protected by Maxims and truck-mounted light guns of the Royal Field Artillery, stood waiting in a siding. As Halfhyde arrived, a tall crane was moving away along the rails: it had just finished its work of hoisting the naval 4.7s onto the specially strengthened trucks and the guns' crews were busy securing the heavy pieces with lashings of rope and wire under the eye of the gunner's mate and the gunnery lieutenant from the *Terrible*. The latter turned at Halfhyde's approach and came across to report the battery loaded and the train ready to move off.

Halfhyde said, 'I await a Mr Bewdley from the secretariat.'

'Bewdley? Never heard of him. What does he want, Halfhyde?'

'I am under orders of secrecy in regard to Mr Bewdley.'

The gunnery lieutenant stared at him. 'I see. Well, it's not up to me to press.' He pulled a watch from his pocket. 'Your Mr Bewdley'll have to look sharp, Halfhyde. The train's due away in five minutes.'

'Yes, indeed. But I'm unable to proceed without Mr Bewdley.'

'I think that'll be up to the Railway Transport Officer, my dear Halfhyde –'

'He also will have orders, I think, to hold the train.'

The lieutenant shrugged. 'If he has, then he has. But he won't be wanting to cause confusion to the time-tables . . . . God knows, Brother Boer's done enough of that already, if in a different sense.'

'Shelling?'

'Yes, and mines too. And ambushes – you know the sort of thing, riflemen at the foot of inclines or in the hills. It'll be no easy ride for you.'

They paced together between the railway lines, in and out of the shadows cast by the moon, already fading a little as the sky began gradually to lighten into an early dawn. The yard was an eerie place, silent in the main, but noisy from time to time as shunting took place and steamy engines chugged and pulled and pushed. Now and again gusts of laughter drifted across from the naval and military gunners or the company of infantry embarked on the armoured train to fight off any Boer attacks. Halfhyde looked at his watch: Bewdley was late. He and the gunnery lieutenant continued pacing and chatting about the war and the curious lack of British progress and as they turned to walk back Halfhyde caught sight of an officer in the uniform of a major, coming from the station offices together with a small, tubby man wearing an incongruous bowler hat.

As the two men approached, Halfhyde saluted the major.

'You're Halfhyde?' the RTO asked.

'I am, sir –'

'Good. This is Mr Bewdley of the secretariat.'

Bewdley extended a hand. 'How do, lieutenant. Ever so sorry . . . for being late. Pray forgive me.'

'You are excused, Mr Bewdley. But now that you're here, we should delay no longer.' Halfhyde's voice was sharp. Aboard his ship he permitted no slackness. 'The consignment –'

'All ticketty-boo, Mr Halfhyde,' Bewdley said cheerfully.

Halfhyde frowned. 'All ticketty-boo' might mean anything at all but he decided to take it at its face value. He was about to speak again when he saw troops, men of the military police, manhandling a creaking cart towards the armoured train.

'That's it,' Bewdley said, waving a hand. 'Straight into the guard's van, all nice and safe.' He lowered his voice. 'Each case marked as gun parts.'

12

'It's to be accompanied by the military police?'

'That's the ticket, Mr Halfhyde, that's the ticket.' Mr Bewdley rubbed his hands together and smiled.

'Do you wish a receipt?' Halfhyde asked. 'And have you any written instructions for me?'

'No to both questions, Mr Halfhyde. I'm coming with you.' Mr Bewdley reached into a pocket and brought out a leather cigar case, which he handed round. He found no acceptances. He thrust a banded cigar into his mouth and struck a match. The RTO and *Terrible*'s gunnery lieutenant took their leave and marched away across the yard in step. Mr Bewdley said, 'Righty-o then, earwig-o as they say.' He chuckled. ''Ere we go, see?'

Halfhyde anticipated an appalling journey. He stalked towards the train, followed by the tubby man, and as the two embarked a whistle shrilled and there was a billow of smoke and steam from the three engines: the train with its guns was heavy, so was double-headed, with the third engine pushing from behind. Slowly at first, then faster, the trucks and carriages moved out for Chieveley and the war zone to the north, and as they pulled away from Cape Town and the sea singing started from the troops.

> 'Goodbye Dolly I must leave you
> Though it breaks my heart to go.
> Something tells me I am needed,
> At the front to fight the foe.
> See, the soldier boys are marching,
> And I can no longer stay –
> Hark! I hear the bugle calling,
> Goodbye Dolly Gray.'

It was poignant enough but, for a seaman, it was an all too military occasion. Halfhyde and Bewdley found themselves in a long drawing-room coach, well furnished, and occupied by a captain and three subalterns of the Royal Scots Fusiliers plus a gunner captain and his two subalterns, with armed soldiers at front and rear, standing guard. The officers' coach, the

13

command coach . . . it felt like something of a royal progress; there were overtones of Her Majesty Queen Victoria travelling from Windsor railway station to Balmoral on Royal Deeside. Halfhyde felt ill at ease; the army officers were polite enough, but cliquish, and the navy was in a minority of one. The talk was all military, of Sir Redvers Buller and Sir George White, of Lieutenant-General Kelly-Kenny's Sixth Division, of Major-General French and Baden-Powell, and an uppish major named Douglas Haig who was determined to push himself forward, of the fighting qualities of the Royal Inniskilling Fusiliers, the Connaught Rangers, the Dublin Fusiliers and the Border Regiment, all of whom formed the Irish Brigade under Brigadier-General Hart.

Halfhyde felt out of the conversation, and no one spoke to Mr Bewdley.

ii

The progress was slow: the heavy train chugged rather than ran. For Halfhyde, boredom set in early, though he made it his business to keep in touch with the naval gun-battery crews by means of clambering along the running-board of the officers' coach, over the linkage and the buffers and along the packed wooden-seated carriages in which the rank and file were travelling. For them it would be a terrible journey, though perhaps easier than a long march. The nights would be cold, the days a hell of scorching sun and blinding dust. They had much distance to cover – around one thousand miles. The railway line did not run direct and there would be changes onto other lines before they reached Chieveley and the environs of Ladysmith.

To Mr Bewdley Halfhyde remarked, 'The military mind is an odd one, I fancy.'

'How's that, Mr Halfhyde?'

'The distance from Durban to Chieveley would have been a fraction of the journey from the Cape. I had the consignment aboard already, on arrival – as you know, of course.' The bullion was never spoken of: it was always 'the consignment'.

14

'Why should I not have retained it, and carried it on by sea to Durban?'

'Ah, now, that's asking.'

'Yes,' Halfhyde said with asperity, 'it is. Do you know the answer, Mr Bewdley?'

The little man pursed his lips. 'Did you by any chance enquire of Captain Wemyss-Buchanan?' He pronounced it Wemiss.

'Yes. He spoke vaguely of wind and weather – possible delays, and the need for speed, it you can call our progress speed.'

Bewdley nodded. 'Then there, most likely, you have it, Mr Halfhyde. The answer.'

'It fails to satisfy me.'

Bewdley's very manner, the way in which he had invoked Wemyss-Buchanan, had aroused Halfhyde's curiosity more than ever, but the tubby man was giving nothing away at all. Halfhyde fumed inside: there was skulduggery at work and a seaman's instinct was all against intrigue and guarded speech. Aboard a ship, be it a merchantman or a Queen's ship, every man knew where he stood and the devious men were always marked and unpopular. But orders were orders, and he would carry them out.

Halfhyde looked at Mr Bewdley, now beginning to drop off to sleep in a corner of the drawing-room coach, his bowler hat tilting slightly. He was never without it on his head so far as Halfhyde had seen. Perhaps it was the symbol of his attainments in life. When not guarding his secrets as to the gold bullion, Mr Bewdley had proved garrulous, talking of his early life at home in London before he had come out to South Africa to enter government service as a clerk with prospects. Mr Bewdley had been a clerk in London, a youth who had started as office boy with a firm of importers and exporters in the City. The high white collar and the black jacket of clerkdom had been Bewdley senior's ambition for the young Horace: his own calling had been that of a railway porter.

'Stationed at Fenchurch Street, Lieutenant Halfhyde,'

Bewdley had said with a nudge, a wink and a gurgle of laughter. '*Stationed* – get it?'

A further joke, though said with sadness, was that his father had been much addicted to the drink known as porter and this had cost him his life: tipsily he had fallen beneath the wheels of a boat train bound for the liners at Tilbury, a train full of nobs in morning dress whose only reaction to the train's stopping had been to pull out their watches anxiously and wonder if the ship would wait, though a few of the ladies had fainted on hearing what had stopped the train. Poor old dad . . . . Mr Bewdley had raised his bowler hat a fraction as he reached the end of the story. He had, it seemed, been fond of his father but knew that the manner of his death would have been fitting in the old man's eyes. Dad had lived for the trains and the serving of the nobs, and would have been quite flattered at being crushed to death by the gentry . . . .

The armoured train moved on through swarms of flies that settled on flesh and bit, moved on through sluggish boredom and the stench from animals lying dead beside the track to become breeding grounds for maggots to turn never-endingly into more flies. The landscape was flat, harsh, waterless and inhospitable, with a distant backdrop of hills. The vegetation was mere scrag; there was the look that said practically nothing would grow and thrive. Halfhyde grew more and more restless, his desire for the sea's freshness mounting by the minute. Mr Bewdley fell asleep and began to snore and stares came from the officers; eyebrows were raised. Mr Bewdley had a peculiarly dreadful snore and he was a civilian, and common. But nobody actually said anything and Mr Bewdley snored on until the gunner captain lifted a glass and dropped it on the floor close by him. The military laughed and Mr Bewdley woke with a start, mopped the sweat from his cheeks and dribble from his chin and said, 'Well, I never did! Thought it was the Boers! Fancy that now.'

iii

'Know anything about bloody Chieveley, do you, mate?'

Victoria had gone ashore, not without rebuke from Edwards, acting in command of the *Glen Halladale* but under no precise orders from Halfhyde to keep the girl confined aboard. He had warned her of danger. Natives could be treacherous and the soldiery was licentious. A young woman on her own might be considered fair game, but Victoria said she could look out for herself. She had addressed her current question to a private of the Argyll and Sutherland Highlanders, a man from Inveraray on Loch Fyne with the wild, dark look of a highlander, who had until recently served at the castle, a gillie to the Duke of Argyll. Victoria found the soldier drinking whisky in a bar.

He wiped the back of a hand across his lips. 'Chieveley . . .'

'Yes. Been there, have you?'

'I've no' been there. But I know of it well. There's been fighting . . . the West Yorks, Devons –'

'Near Ladysmith, isn't it?'

'Aye. In range o' the Boer guns.'

She asked directly, 'How do I get there, mate?'

The Scot grinned. 'If ye've any sense at all, ye dinna!'

'Look, I want to get there. I have a – a friend there.'

'Soldier?'

She shook her head. 'No. Navy. He's gone with some guns, I reckon.'

'A naval brigade.' The Scot called for another whisky. He offered to buy one for Victoria, but she refused. 'Ye'll no' get yersel' intae a war zone, lassie, nae a hope in hell without a better reason. An' I've a strong feeling your friend would no' be wanting you to.'

'Dead right,' she said. 'But if you were a woman – and if you wanted to get to Chieveley – how would you go about it, eh?'

The Scot shrugged. 'Given all the ifs,' he said, 'an' if I were gyte enough –'

'Gyte?'

'Crazy. Weel, I'd join an ambulance train – if there was one going that way.'

'Ambulance train? That means nurses, eh? But I'm no nurse.'

17

'Nor d'ye need to be, lassie. There's always room for volunteers to help the wounded. Just someone to make hersel' useful.'

She nodded, a distant look in her eyes. 'Thanks for the tip, mate,' she said. 'But there's a bloody snag, isn't there? I only want to go to bloody Chieveley, nowhere else. I reckon they'd smell a bloody rat once I said that.'

Nevertheless, the Scot had given her the glimmering of an idea. She made her way back to the *Glen Halladale*: while ashore with her the day before, Halfhyde had attended to the deficiencies of her wardrobe. Her long-ago pierhead jump at Devonport, in effect a stowing away, had left her poorly provided. Here in Cape Town she would create no good impression by looking like a waif and stray as she did now. But aboard the ship she had a pretty dress and a hat with a veil.

iv

The armoured train had been shifted to another line at De Aar Junction and again at Rosmead Junction and was heading towards Burgersdorp and the Orange River. Now they were close to the enemy and everyone was alert for trouble, the infantry and gunners standing to.

Halfhyde had a word with his guns' crews. To Petty Officer Dunning he said, 'I have personal orders. My action station is to be the guard's van – I can tell you no more than that. But if there are casualties, I am to be informed and I may take the decision to act as a replacement.'

'Aye, aye, sir.' The gunner's mate saluted and turned away to his guns' crews crouched ready with their rifles behind the sandbags and side armour. Halfhyde clambered back to the running-board of the guard's van and went in through the opened door, sliding it shut behind him. Bewdley was there, with the military police guard under a sergeant. The air was close and foetid and here too sandbags lined the sides. The bullion was piled in the middle of the van, anonymous in its wooden cases marked as gun parts. Obviously there would have been the fullest possible secrecy about the movement of the gold but there could always be a slip. Bewdley had spoken, when they were alone together, of the possibility of Boer spies in Cape Town, perhaps even within the secretariat itself. They could never be entirely sure. If anything had leaked, the gold would be a target for Boer intentions and any attack would be made in strength and with purpose, going beyond the usual harassment by the mounted farmers with rifles. Mr Bewdley was looking agitated, much worried about the gold that was his personal responsibility still.

Halfhyde said, 'A new experience for you, I take it.'

'Yes – yes, indeed it is, Lieutenant Halfhyde. I've not been in the war zone until now.'

'No more have I, Mr Bewdley.'

'Ah, not out here perhaps. But you're of the navy and used to it.'

'In theory only. Much of the Empire has been at peace these many years. There'll not be a man out here who has ever faced war until now, apart from those who've served on the North-West Frontier of India.'

'Yes, that's true, to be sure.'

'So you're not alone, Mr Bewdley.'

The armoured train rumbled on along the track, swaying from side to side. It was dusk now; one of the military policemen lit a paraffin lantern and hung it from a hook in the van's roof. Smoke issued until the man trimmed the wick down. The atmosphere grew more and more close. Bewdley, sitting on the floor, was huddled with his back against the bullion cases as though protectively. Halfhyde had gathered that the conveyance of the gold was Bewdley's personal triumph, the accolade of trust after many years of service. Bewdley was a simple clerk no longer: he held the rank of an assistant deputy principal in the Cape secretariat, but even so, the bullion was a very special duty. Halfhyde grinned inwardly: he had a vision of Bewdley, if the worst happened, standing firmly spread-eagled before the bullion, blood-stained bandage around his forehead beneath the bowler hat, showing the Empire's defiance to the Boer, a kind of Custer's Last Stand transferred to the South African veldt. Then he suffered a twinge of conscience: one should not mock a sense of duty nor titter at figures of comic appearance when they exhibited it.

The train swayed on through the night and crossed into the Orange Free State over a ramshackle bridge spanning the Orange River. The bridge was known to be in British hands: Halfhyde heard cheering from outside, and opened the door of the van. A moon was up now, and in its light he could see kilted Scots on guard. He heard a shouted exchange between the troops along the track and the infantry captain commanding the train. He closed the door.

Bewdley asked, 'What was that, Lieutenant Halfhyde?'

'Information that the Boers are a few miles ahead, or are believed to be.'

The little man nodded and wiped his face with his handkerchief. His fingers shook and he huddled closer to the stacked cases. Halfhyde fancied he was debating something within his head; there was an anxious frown and a look of uncertainty. Ten minutes later there was a loud shout from one of the gun-carriage trucks ahead.

'Enemy ahead, left and right o' the track!'

Once again Halfhyde slid the van door open and hung from the entry, looking ahead. He saw shadowy forms, mounted men riding down from the north. As he shut the door he heard the first of the firing, heard a quickly-torn-off cry from one of the trucks in the leading section of the train.

Bewdley said in a high voice, 'Oh, my goodness me.'

The train was increasing speed now; Halfhyde hoped the extra strain wouldn't finish off the panting, overworked engines. There was more firing, a barrage of rifles that grew heavier, and the troops were firing back. There was a sustained rattle from the Maxims through the gun-ports in the armour at each end of the train. More screams came and bullets thudded into the sandbagged sides of the guard's van. The train was rocking now. One of the bullion cases slid from the top of the pile and crashed to the floor, splitting open. The dullness of the bullion showed; there was a whistle from the army sergeant.

Mr Bewdley scrambled to his feet and assisted by one of the military policemen, heaved the broken case back into place, warning the soldiers never to speak of the bullion. He was sweating like a pig, his starched collar wilting badly. Two bullets took the door and came through, one of them sending Mr Bewdley's bowler hat spinning from his head and causing him to give a squeak of fear.

Halfhyde felt a mounting impatience with his orders to remain with the gold while the naval ratings were exposed to concentrated fire; and he decided the time had come to disregard those orders. He opened the door, took the running-board with his feet, and edged perilously along towards the 4.7s in their trucks, paying no attention to Mr Bewdley's protests or the Boers' bullets.

He reached the first truck.

'Well, Dunning?'

'All's well, sir. No casualties.' The bearded petty officer was standing by with his gun's crew at the firing points between the sandbags. The naval guns were not fitted up for action: whilst aboard the train they were mere cargo, too heavy to be fired; their role would come after they had been disembarked at Chieveley. Dunning had scarcely spoken when one of the ratings gave a choking cry and spun round clutching at his throat, then falling heavily in a crumpled heap. Halfhyde went to him and felt for the heart. There was a faint flicker, and then even that stopped. His face hard, Halfhyde took up the man's rifle and went to his place at the firing point. He thrust the rifle through, squinted along the sights and fired at a thickset rider close by. His aim was good: the Boer crashed sideways, caught his feet in the dangling reins and was dragged along the rough, stony ground. The train went on amid clouds of smoke and steam. A number of men fell to the track, arms flung up as the Boer marksmen, keeping pace easily with the train, sprayed it with bullets. Halfhyde swore aloud: the troops hadn't a proper chance – there was not room enough for every man to return the fire. They were hamstrung in a sense, sacrifices to a lack of thought by the high command, while the Boer riders had all the freedom in the world in which to fight and manoeuvre, to slaughter virtually sitting targets whenever heads appeared at the firing points.

The running battle went on seemingly without end. But after some twenty minutes the nature of the terrain came to the train's assistance: they met a downward incline, not very much but enough to give the engines a chance, and the train accelerated and at last drew away from the riders.

Dunning said, 'They're giving up, sir.'

Halfhyde nodded. 'For my money, there'll be more of them ahead.'

'I'd not be surprised at that, sir.'

As the Boers fell away behind, the infantry captain was seen coming along the running-boards from the front end of the train. He dropped down into the naval truck, asking about casualties.

'One man dead,' Halfhyde reported.

'I'm sorry. There have been too many casualties, more than is normal.' The captain pulled at his walrus moustache and stared at Halfhyde. He was a cadaverous man and smart as paint in his khaki and Sam Browne, but there was a military superciliousness about him that grated on Halfhyde. 'There must be a reason – don't you think?'

Halfhyde shrugged. 'No doubt. There usually is.'

'Those cases that came aboard with you?'

'Gun parts, as marked.'

'Gun parts my bottom! Gun parts don't go with a military police escort, a naval officer, and a blasted civilian from the secretariat. It's my bet Brother Boer knows something that I don't know – and you do.'

Halfhyde shrugged again. 'I have no knowledge of anything beyond the markings, Captain Ross, and –'

'Damn it, man, I don't believe you. I want to know the facts and I want to know them now.' There was a blaze in his eyes, visible in the moon's light, and a hand had gone to the holstered revolver at his side. 'I command this train and I'm giving you an order, Lieutenant Halfhyde –'

'You give me no orders,' Halfhyde said coolly. 'My orders are from the Admiral commanding at the Cape –'

'Who is not here. I am.'

'Indeed you are. But you shall not come between me and my duty. If you force me into considerations of relative rank, may I remind you that a captain of infantry ranks with but *after* a lieutenant in Her Majesty's fleet and thus I am your senior officer. Also, this is to some extent a naval train as well as a military one.'

'You shall –'

'I have nothing further to say, Captain Ross.' Halfhyde saw the anger and frustration in the officer's face, saw the way his hands were clenching and unclenching, saw the evidence of a nervous strain, the strain no doubt of weeks of war, of taking trains through hostile territory, and he relented. He placed a hand on Ross's shoulder. He said, 'Before I was called back into naval service I commanded a ship of my own in the merchant service, and I have also held command of torpedo-boat destroyers. I would perhaps have reacted in the same way as yourself . . . but I am bound to follow my orders. I think you will understand.'

Captain Ross gave no answer; turning his back on Halfhyde he moved farther down the train. Some minutes later he came back, on his way forward to the officers' coach. Halfhyde asked about the wounded men. There was, he knew, no medical man aboard the train.

Ross said coldly, 'They must wait for Chieveley.'

'And the dead?'

'The same applies. I can't stop for burial parties, surely you realize that?'

Many of the dead had been left behind; their retrieval couldn't delay the train either. Meanwhile there was some way yet to go to the railway station at Chieveley and with the next dawn would come the sun and the day's mounting heat. Back along the railway line the carrion birds would have a field day. In the armoured trucks and carriages the troops and naval guns' crews would suffer the stench.

v

Dressed like a lady, Victoria Penn went down the gangway from the *Glen Halladale*, all Edwards' warnings ringing in her ears. She insisted she would be all right; and she would, she said mendaciously, be back aboard before dark, or anyway before the ship sailed for Durban next day.

'But if it's not to be before dark, where will you –'

She cut in. 'Look, I found friends when I went ashore this morning. A digger and his wife I used to know in Sydney. They got a house here in Cape Town. I'll be all right, see?' She gave the first mate her urchin grin. 'Reckon I'll be safer with me mates than with a bunch of women-starved sailors, right?'

She went; she regretted the need to lie; Mr Edwards, he'd been a good bloke but if she'd told the truth he'd have kept her aboard by force most probably. She also regretted the fact that she was totally friendless in Cape Town and had no idea in the world where she was going to spend the night other than perhaps in some cheap hotel – or the Salvation Army hostel, which would be even cheaper and much safer.

Meanwhile it wasn't the Salvation Army she saw all around her as she left the docks and its forest of masts and yards and once again came into the town itself. If one attempt was made to pick her up, there were a dozen. English, Scots, Irish, Canadians, New Zealanders, Australians. Never mind the fine dress; she was still Victoria Penn, no lady. She walked on disdainfully, swinging a parasol, head held high. Her intention was to make for the railway station and wait there, making enquiries about hospital trains leaving for the war zone. She wouldn't mention Chieveley; but if she picked up word about a train bound for there, then she would insinuate herself. That highland soldier had said – more or less – that young ladies would always be welcome aboard the hospital trains.

Well then, they wouldn't ask too many questions. You didn't look a gift horse in the mouth. As for herself, she wasn't worried about the danger. More about the relative chances of success or failure. Maybe she wouldn't find St Vincent Halfhyde, but at

24

least she would be near him if he wanted her, and if she could get to know he needed her. There couldn't be all that many naval officers in a land war and when she began asking around in Chieveley the word would soon get through.

She went on towards the railway station, with no reason to believe that anyone might be taking an interest in her, never realizing that two men had seen her leave the docks and, taking advantage of a stroke of luck, had thereafter kept a discreet distance behind her. They were there when she entered the station; they saw her saunter up to a booking office, where she appeared to be making an enquiry; they saw her go from there to the ladies' waiting-room, where she vanished for some minutes and then came out to approach an army officer outside the Railway Transport Office. They saw her disappointed look. They saw her leave the station and walk somewhat aimlessly along the street. They saw her hailed by a kilted Scot wearing the badges of the Argyll and Sutherland Highlanders and they saw her stop and talk and then go with the Scot into a bar.

THREE

A sudden heavy jolt as though the engine had run into buffers had thrown men off their feet throughout the length of the armoured train. There was a roar of escaping steam and the red glow of fires from ahead, where the leading engine lay toppled and broken, its furnace spilling out through the stokehole, the driver and fireman screaming as they were taken by the red-hot coals. The second engine lay at an angle and two of the leading trucks had come off the track, which was itself twisted.

Halfhyde and the others in the guard's van were thrown violently against the sides and the bullion cases slid about the floor, the neat pile toppled into chaos and mixed with dislodged sandbags. Rifle fire was heard, coming from all sides, it seemed.

Then Halfhyde heard Captain Ross shouting, 'Get the men out, sar'nt-major! All out and take cover beneath the train!'

Halfhyde said, 'We stay here, all of us. We remain as close guard on the cases.'

The military police sergeant was inclined to demur. 'Sir! The captain's orders –'

'You'll take my orders from now, sergeant. We have a particular duty – I think Mr Bewdley will agree – on behalf of the secretariat, the civil power.'

'Yes indeed, Lieutenant Halfhyde.' Bewdley was shaking all over as he lurched to his feet and retrieved his bowler hat; there were no more jokes, no more puns left in him now. He was face to face with war and he was pale with terror. 'But what do we do? I ask you!'

Halfhyde gave a grim, humourless laugh. 'We shoot any man who attempts to enter the guard's van, Mr Bewdley, and if necessary I shall inform Captain Ross of the facts – the time may have come for that, I fancy.'

'It is not to be divulged on any –'

'Yes, I'm aware of that. But things change, and the man on the spot sometimes has to change with them – but we shall see. In the meantime, Mr Bewdley, you stand in personal danger. I –'

He broke off as suddenly the van's door was opened from the outside and an NCO heaved himself up.

'All out, sir, was the captain's orders – *if* you please, sir.'

'My compliments to Captain Ross,' Halfhyde said, 'and I'm remaining at my post, under orders of the Admiral at the Cape. Tell me what's happened, corporal.'

'Ambush, sir.' The NCO's voice was hoarse, hurried. 'Bloody Boers, sir – bloody great boulder on the track round a bend with a rock overhang. Leading engine's bust, sir.' He disappeared.

'So we shan't move again,' Halfhyde said from the darkness; he had doused the hanging oil-lamp by this time. He spoke to the MP sergeant. 'Is the cart all right, sergeant?'

'Yes, sir. Far as I can feel, that is, sir.'

'Well, that's something. At least we have transport!'

Bewdley gave a high sound as if verging on hysteria. 'Transport!'

'Wheels, Mr Bewdley. If necessary we shall *push* the consignment to Chieveley!'

Halfhyde felt the thud of bullets into the woodwork of the van; all the men were now flat on the floor, with the rifles aimed at the sliding doors, now securely bolted, on either side. No Boer would enter while one man lived, but if the fire was kept up from outside then, finally, they would all be killed. That firing was intense and sustained from both sides. It was obvious that the Boers were there in force and might well have many reserves to call upon. Halfhyde called for Bewdley in the pitch dark.

'I'm here, Lieutenant Halfhyde.' The voice came from

Halfhyde's left and he reached out a hand and found the civilian's shoulder. He shifted himself closer.

'A word in your ear, Mr Bewdley.'

'Yes?'

The racket from outside was enough to drown speech, so Halfhyde spoke with his lips against Bewdley's ear. 'A little while ago I said you were in personal danger. So are we all. But perhaps you take my point?'

'I think I do, Lieutenant Halfhyde, yes.'

'You alone are in possession of certain knowledge.'

'Yes indeed –'

'The time has come to share it with me. If you die –'

'Yes.' Bewdley was clearly anxious. 'Dear me, this is a dilemma I do declare, Lieutenant Halfhyde! My orders were precise, you see. Nothing was to be divulged.'

'Not even in extremity?'

'I was never given the authority to do so.'

Breath hissed through Halfhyde's teeth. 'But you are a senior civil servant, Mr Bewdley.'

'Middling senior, yes.'

'Senior enough to make your own decisions when faced with the need to do so, I think. In my view the need is here. You should not delay.' As if to give point to his words there was a heavy blow against the woodwork of the right-hand door, like the blow of an axe. One of the soldiers fired with the barrel of his rifle against the door, and there was a broken-off cry from outside.

'Come, Mr Bewdley. I demand the orders. Damn it, man, I'd have had to know ultimately in any case!'

'Yes . . . .'

'Then for God's sake tell me, or I shall shake the words from you!' Halfhyde spoke through set teeth, and tightened his grip on the civilian's shoulder, infuriated now by the little man's obstinacy.

'Yes, very well,' Bewdley said in immense agitation. 'Mind, I may not have been entrusted with the full information . . . . I have a feeling I have not. But this I can tell you, Lieutenant

Halfhyde: the consignment will be met at Chieveley by an escort of guns and infantry and taken north into the Drakensberg –'

'The mountains bordering Natal?'

'Yes, that's right.' Mr Bewdley hesitated, suddenly and for no apparent reason starting to shake again and to look extremely emotional and upset. He went on, 'There'll be a man called . . . called van Buren with the –'

'Van Buren? Dutch? A Boer?'

'Dutch, yes, but not –'

'Why? What has a Dutchman to do with British gold, Mr Bewdley?'

Once again the little man seemed to hesitate, then said, 'I understand he's often been of assistance to the government at the Cape, Lieutenant Halfhyde. At a very high level. I have never myself come into direct contact with him, but he's well spoken for and is trusted although I myself believe him to be a kind of – of adventurer –'

'Out for himself?'

'Very likely, yes. A superior soldier of fortune –'

'And his connection with the consignment?'

'He is to act as guide to the escort, into the Drakensberg. That is all I know at this moment . . . . There will be more information waiting at Chieveley.'

'So you don't know the destination?'

'No, I don't, I'm afraid, not the final destination . . . .'

'And all this has been arranged by the government at the Cape?'

'Yes indeed, Lieutenant Halfhyde. At the highest level I may say.'

'And the Commander-in-Chief?'

'I understand it's being done with the full approval of General Buller.'

Halfhyde was about to comment on this when there was the shattering sound of a heavy field-gun from some distance away. Within seconds Halfhyde heard the high whine of a shell passing directly overhead and almost immediately after there was a huge explosion at the rear of the armoured train. The guard's van rocked violently and the ground seemed to heave up. Through the holes made in the sides by the Boer riflemen a brilliant flash of light had been seen, followed by a red glow. As Halfhyde rolled across the van's floor there was a second explosion and the bullion cases flew through the air as the van toppled from the track to fetch up on its side.

ii

'So ye're no' away for Chieveley yet,' the Scot said as he came up to Victoria.

'Doesn't bloody look like it, does it?'

The Scot grinned. 'It does not, I agree. What did they tell you at the railway, then?'

'They said, if I wanted to join an ambulance train, I'd have to make myself fully available to the military authorities and maybe they'd allocate me.' Victoria sniffed. 'No bloody go, mate! I only want to get to bloody Chieveley.'

'Aye, so you said, lass. Come now – a dram'll do ye no harm while you put on your thinking cap again.' The Scot seemed already a little drunk; he took Victoria's arm. 'Come on into the saloon, eh?'

'Ladies,' Victoria said, 'don't bloody go into saloons.'

'Wheesht! Earlier you –'

'But I'm no bloody lady,' she said impishly, 'and I reckon I could do with a gin.'

'Fine.' The Scot – his name, he said, was Angus MacGill – held open the door of the bar and they went in. MacGill called for whisky, and gin for the lady. The place was packed with troops and seamen and the two were crushed against the bar. MacGill was looking around as if for a friend. There just might, he said, be someone who could help, a man maybe from a medical detail who could give her some information about the likelihood of there being an ambulance train for Chieveley, and who might even help to get her enlisted aboard it. But the Scot soon lost interest in that aspect; one whisky followed another down a thirsty and capacious throat and between whiskies he

30

joined in the singing that was shattering the air of the bar. In an increasingly slurred voice he roared out the words:

> 'We're soldiers of the Queen, my lads,
> We've been, my lads, we've seen, my lads,
> We're part o' *Scotland*'s glory, lads,
> For we're soldiers of the Queen . . . .'

He put both arms around Victoria, held her tight, and kissed her on somewhat startled lips. Coolly she straightened the hat Halfhyde had bought her the day before.

'Thanks very much', she said, 'for the gin. Now I'll be off before you forget you're a gentleman, Mr MacGill.'

She turned and began shoving her way through the crowd. A hefty hand made a grab for her from behind. She stopped and swung round into MacGill's arms once again.

'You're a bloody trier, I'll say that,' she said, freed her right arm from the crush, and brought her palm stingingly across the Scot's face. He let out a roar of rage but his arms were seized by two bluejackets who held onto him while Victoria made her escape.

Outside the bar were the two men who had noticed her exit from the dockyard. One of them raised a wide-brimmed bush hat.

'Miss Penn?' he asked politely.

'Well, that's me all right. Who's asking?'

'Name of Flannery. You've come off the *Glen Halladale*, isn't that right, Miss Penn?'

'Why, yes.' Temper flared. 'Just you don't bloody tell me! That bloody first mate sent you to bring me back aboard, has he?'

The two men exchanged a brief glance. 'Why, yes, that's right. You'd best come with us, Miss Penn, or that first mate, he'll bring in the police and there'll be a fuss.'

The speaker looked around; a cab was moving slowly past, behind a sad-looking horse. Victoria, with tears of fury pricking at her eyes, was propelled aboard as it stopped. They set off towards the docks; but before they had got that far the cab was halted at the head of a sleazy dockland street of half-derelict houses and some gold was transferred into the hand of the Kaffir driver. The men got down, holding Victoria fast. She felt the hard muzzle of a revolver pressing into her side. She opened her mouth to scream; immediately a hand came down hard across her lips. She bit it, and the man gave a sharp cry and the revolver pressed in cruelly.

'Don't try that again, Miss Penn.'

She gave a shiver of fear and looked around. The cab-horse was trotting away and there was no one else around as she was taken into the side street. A scream would have been wasted. Victoria cursed to herself as she was manhandled along: she'd dropped herself right in it, making the men's task the easier by mentioning Edwards. If she hadn't jumped to a stupid conclusion she might have found willing assistance in the bar she had only just left. But she had seen no reason to be suspicious . . . .

She asked, 'What do you bloody want with me, eh?'

'You'll find out. Just keep your trap shut, Miss Penn, and you won't get hurt.'

She stumbled on uneven ground; it was little more than a trodden dirt track, fringed by unsalubrious hovels. As they penetrated deeper, there were signs of life. Black faces peered from doorways, there was the cry of a baby, and through an alley between two of the hovels Victoria caught a glimpse of children playing in a filthy yard. The men were on either side of her. She believed they were English; there was no Dutch accent anyway, and they hadn't seemed to have the South African accent either. Flannery? That was Irish. Was there some connection with the past, the fairly long past now – that arms cargo out of Sydney for Queenstown in County Cork, embarked as cased machine parts and protected by the guns of Porteous Higgins and the man Gaboon, finally beaten in their schemes by St Vincent Halfhyde?

Surely not. By this time Higgins had been hanged in England; and Gaboon had died in Galway City, riddled with bullets from Irishmen whom he and Higgins had tried to double-cross . . . .

Flannery. Probably not the man's real name in any case.

Towards the end of the long street, Victoria was taken into one of the hovels, a filthy place that smelled of rotting vegetables and waste of all kinds. She was taken into a back room where an old crone sat in a rocking chair, her face wizened and gums toothless, her lips moving in a chewing motion without cease. There was a man in the room as well, a short, square man with a face scarred from his right eye to the corner of his mouth. The face was evil, and was made more so when he smiled.

He said, 'So here you are.' He looked at the man who called himself Flannery. 'Quick work, sure enough! How'd you manage it?'

Flannery told him, and added, 'She's expected back aboard. We'll have to move fast –'

'She'll never be looked for here.'

'Best not take too many chances, Mahon.'

The man didn't answer that. He came across from where he had been standing, leaning against the wall. He stopped in front of Victoria and stood with his arms akimbo; powerful arms, with very thick wrists. He said, 'We meet again, but in reversed roles.'

'I've never met you.'

He smiled; the teeth were black stumps, his breath sickened her. 'Not met perhaps. But I've seen you. My God, I've seen you . . . the Captain's woman, aboard the *Glen Halladale*. Remember? It's only a few weeks ago.'

She caught her breath. 'The convicts –'

'The draft from Her Majesty's prison of Dartmoor, yes –'

'But they were all taken into the army when we got here to Cape Town!'

'Correct. But me and my mates here – the military aren't so hot as the screws at Dartmoor, Miss Penn. It wasn't hard to get away, believe me, and with a little outside help to set us up they'll never find us again. Nor will they ever find you, Miss Penn. Just bear that in mind. And think of this too: you're no

33

longer the high and mighty Captain's woman, flaunting herself from the poop before a hundred convicts with chains upon their bodies and guarded by armed warders.' He reached out and took her chin in his hand, a rough, coarse hand with warts upon it. She felt sickness and fear rise together. 'You're one of us now, Miss Penn. And you'll do as you're told. First thing is, you'll tell us what we want to know.'

She said nothing, but stared into his face, feeling the heavy beat of her heart.

'Aboard the *Glen Halladale* there was talk of gold. We know it was there . . . a hundred thousand pounds sterling, so the word went.'

She said, 'It's gone now. It's in government hands.'

There was a nod. 'Yes, we know that too. But we hear it's not going to remain in Cape Town. I spoke of outside help, Miss Penn. A hundred thousand pounds goes a long way – or the promise of it does. In certain circumstances the value may exceed that many times. It depends on what use the gold is to be put to and where it has gone. And that is what I want to know.'

She managed a laugh. 'Don't ask me! How should I bloody know?'

'Then I'll ask you a different question: where has Captain Halfhyde gone?'

'He's in the navy now, Royal Naval Reserve. He takes naval orders now. He doesn't tell me what they are.'

'No? Think again, Miss Penn. Halfhyde was much concerned personally with the gold bullion. You know that.'

'Yes,' she said. 'An attempt at bribery and it didn't come off. That's his only connection with it. It's in Government hands and he's on naval service.'

'Then tell me where he's gone on naval service. We know that he's left the *Glen Halladale* and that the ship is in the hands of the first mate for passage to Durban. It's likely enough Halfhyde will rejoin her there. I want to know what he's doing between Cape Town and Durban, and where he's doing it. And you're going to tell me.'

'I don't know where he's gone.'

34

The man looked aside at the other two. 'Hold her fast,' he said.

His hand came up, took her a couple of stinging blows across the face, left and right. She reeled; her bottom lip was split and blood was running. 'That's just for a start, Miss Penn,' he said.

iii

'Are you all right, Mr Bewdley?'

'I'm all right, Lieutenant Halfhyde.' He sounded out of breath, and somewhat shaky. 'Only by the grace of God, I fancy . . . . There is much blood.'

'But not yours, I think. One of these poor fellows . . .'

The side of the van had been shattered and was now above their heads and red light from fires was coming through. Halfhyde, in that angry, flickering light, could see the extent of the injuries. As the pile of bullion cases had been thrown about one of them had come down on the head of the military police sergeant, splitting it open; and the man's body was lying across Bewdley, who was pinned to the downward side of the van, now flat on the ground and forming the floor. A lance-corporal was lying dazed, with a leg twisted up beneath his body, while another man lay in a corner with an obviously broken neck. The heavy gunfire appeared to have ceased but there was still sporadic rifle fire overlying yells and cries.

Halfhyde freed Bewdley then climbed to the jagged aperture in the wooden side and looked out. He saw British uniforms advancing over some rising land, clearly outlined in the light from a railway carriage set ablaze by the artillery shells. There was cheering as a sudden surge forward on the part of the British troops brought a field gun into view over the rise and, leaving a number of dead behind, the Boer riflemen began streaming away towards the west, pursued by gunfire.

Halfhyde heard Bewdley's voice. 'What is it, Lieutenant Halfhyde?'

'A battery of the field artillery, I fancy, arrived to scatter the Boers.'

'Praise be to God,' Mr Bewdley said. He was feeling himself

all over; he appeared to be intact by some miracle but he was desperately worried about the bullion, which was strewn everywhere, the cases split wide open. Together with those of the military police who were uninjured, working in the light from outside, he began pushing the consignment into some sort of order and carrying out a count of the bars. Halfhyde jumped down to lend a hand, wondering how in heaven's name they were to get the gold to Chieveley now: despite his earlier words to Bewdley that if necessary they would push it, he doubted if to do so would be possible through hostile territory; and in any case the cart was now lying on its side with a wheel off and the bottom planking split.

There was a sound from outside, a sound as of someone climbing up the broken woodwork, and a head appeared. It was Captain Ross of the Royal Scots Fusiliers.

'Gold,' he said in a flat voice. 'So that's what it was!'

'Gold indeed – and my apologies for being unable to inform you.' Halfhyde paused. 'We now have a problem: how to get the gold to Chieveley. I take it the train won't run any further!'

Ross said, 'I will send a runner to Chieveley, with a request for another train.'

'How far to Chieveley?' Halfhyde asked.

'About twenty miles.'

'And us in the role of sitting ducks, awaiting more Boer attacks. Meanwhile, the bullion's vitally important to the government at the Cape, and –'

'What exactly are you asking for?'

Halfhyde said, 'An escort to Chieveley, and as soon as possible. There's a cart – damaged but I think not beyond repair –'

'A handcart, over this kind of country?'

'Needs must.' Halfhyde shrugged. 'Those of us who have served at sea are well accustomed to improvising, and I believe I can get the bullion to Chieveley so long as the Boers permit –'

Ross interrupted. 'I can't spare men for an escort, Halfhyde. We must remain together to fight off attacks until a train is sent through from Chieveley. I'm sorry.'

'Why not march your men out, and reach Chieveley faster than waiting for a response to your runner?'

Ross scowled; he was still angry about Halfhyde's earlier withholding of information. He said abruptly, 'You forget the train and the guns. Neither the guns nor the engines must fall into the hands of the Boers. They'll be recovered when a repair gang reaches us, and I must wait.'

'I see,' Halfhyde said. 'In that case, I shall detach my seamen gunners from their guns and march with them as escort to the gold, to Chieveley.'

iv

Ross had argued, had even given an order that Halfhyde was to remain aboard the train. Halfhyde had repeated that rank for rank he was the senior and he intended to do precisely what he had said. He passed the word to Dunning to fall the seamen in, and then they marched away with the handcart, given a quick makeshift repair.

The going was hard for men more accustomed to moving about wooden decks in bare feet. The moon shining down on the lonely land lit their way; but later, with an hour to go to the dawn, the moon became shadowed by some heavy and unusual cloud and the guns' crews marched in almost total darkness across the veldt with their rifles ready, every man alert for trouble. Attack could come at any moment and might not be seen until it was too late. The Boer farmers knew their land well and had already become expert at concealment and surprise attack; and Halfhyde knew that his seamen were likely enough to prove remarkably unhandy in land fighting. Seamen were for one thing not trained for the surprise attack: aboard a ship there were no enemies and though the bridge might have to cope in war with the sudden appearance of a hostile ship over the horizon, the lower deck had merely to obey the call to action and wait for the order for the guns to open. And the land was ghostly; strange shapes loomed, scrub and trees and bushes, and the occasional thicket lay across the track as likely camouflage for Boer riflemen. Halfhyde marched in the lead

37

with the handcart trundling behind him in Mr Bewdley's charge, heavily guarded by the seamen. With Halfhyde was a lance-bombardier detached as guide from the field battery that had relieved the broken train's personnel. This man knew the route and the terrain well. On his advice the naval party marched in as much silence as was possible; sounds carried clear across the veldt and could reach listening Boer ears. By Halfhyde's order there was no talking, but the creaking of the handcart and the jingle of leather straps and their attached accoutrements could not be prevented.

A cold wind sprang up and there were muttered curses from the marching men; Mr Bewdley turned up his coat collar and moved doggedly on, the picture of misery beside the handcart, uttering an occasional 'God bless my soul' as his feet slid from under him on the rough ground and he was heaved upright again by the strong arm of a seaman.

When the dawn came the wind fell away again; according to their guide fourteen miles still lay ahead to Chieveley.

'We must count our blessings,' Halfhyde said. 'Six miles covered and no attack!' With any luck the gold could now reach Chieveley in safety; every step took them closer to the British positions, and the Boer attentions would be mainly concentrated on the ground between Ladysmith and the Tugela.

But after Chieveley, what?

Why was the Cape secretariat handing over gold bullion to a Dutchman, whatever his standing was said to be? That question still remained to be answered. Halfhyde could see no light but remained convinced that something dirty had been handed to him, even though it was highly unlikely that Sir Redvers Buller would lend his name and approval to anything underhand.

Halfhyde marched on, his thoughts moving restlessly through his mind. He was brought back to his surroundings by the guide.

'Someone away to the right, sir!'

Halfhyde started, and looked towards where the lance-bombardier was pointing. He saw a solitary horseman, still some distance off, riding towards the naval party.

The lance-bombardier said, 'I don't think he's wearing uniform, sir.'

'A Boer?'

'Yes, sir. But he looks to be alone, sir.'

'Then why is he approaching us?' Halfhyde moved aside, turned and called to the gunner's mate marching in rear of the escort. 'Petty Officer Dunning?'

'Sir?'

'Stand-to, but nothing hostile unless I give the order.'

They moved on, rifles ready in their hands as the lone rider closed in.

FOUR

The thickset man, the one who had been addressed as Mahon, had continued with his face slapping and had then used his fists; Victoria's face was bruised and bleeding, but she was giving nothing away. She spat at the man. He hit back viciously.

'You're going to talk. Don't imagine you're not. There's plenty of things that can be done to a woman. I'll be doing them.' He ripped at her clothing, baring small, tight breasts. He spoke to the men holding Victoria. She was dragged across the dirty floor – it was bare earth – and laid face down across a table. The clothing was dragged from her body. One of the men had a sjambok. It came down cruelly, again and again. Her body was badly lacerated, the flesh felt as if it were on fire. She screamed, and a hand was clamped across her mouth. The beating continued.

Mahon said, 'Talk or it goes on. When you're ready to talk, just nod your head.'

She struggled furiously, writhing and contorting, but she couldn't evade the sjambok. Tears streamed; the indignity was as bad as the lash. In the corner of the room the old crone mouthed silently and stared; she was obviously terrified and too decrepit to move, too transfixed even to utter. Victoria would not give in. But she could probably gain some respite by giving the man a false destination, even though she would suffer for it later. She was about to give a nod and say that Halfhyde was bound for Mafeking when there was a bang at the outer

40

door and Mahon dropped the sjambok and stood waiting while one of the others went out of the room.

He came back with another man, a tall man, smartly dressed and with an authoritative air about him. He took the scene in with a sweeping glance.

'What is this?' he asked, speaking with no more than a trace of an Afrikaner accent. 'Who is the woman?'

'Halfhyde's woman, Mr Pieters.'

'I never sanctioned beatings such as this.'

Mahon said, 'Well, I'm sorry, but we have to know where Halfhyde –'

'We do know. This was not necessary, had you waited a little. I have information that Halfhyde is on his way to Chieveley in Natal. Now you will stop this brutality.'

Mahon scowled but said, 'As you say, Mr Pieters. But the woman must come with us now.'

'Yes. Transport will be here shortly. We shall wait.'

ii

Halfhyde halted the handcart and its escort as the rider came up, his hands held high in peace, his horse moving only slowly.

Halfhyde called out, 'Who are you and what do you want?'

The man smiled genially. He was heavily bearded, square and strong-looking. In a heavily accented voice he said, 'My name is Koornhof.'

'A Boer?'

'No. I am from Amsterdam. I come in friendship. You are Lieutenant Halfhyde of the naval reserve?'

Halfhyde stared up into the man's face. 'How do you know that, may I ask?'

'I recognize the badges of rank, and I was expecting you. I represent the one whom you were to meet at Chieveley – Jan van Buren –'

'You seem to know a lot, Mr Koornhof. But how did you know you would find me here? I was expected at Chieveley, aboard the armoured train!'

'True. But there is such a thing as the bush telegraph . . . .

41

The Kaffirs are very willing to co-operate in exchange for favours, you know.' Despite the accent, the English was impeccable. 'Often the bush telegraph is faster than either the runner or your army's field telegraph, where it exists. Word of what had happened reached Chieveley, and the plans were changed in the interest of secrecy. I rode out towards where the damaged train was reported – frankly I didn't expect to come upon you on the way, but since I have done so all is well and a little time can now be saved.' Koornhof laughed breezily. 'I think you do not understand even now?'

'Yes, I do. But why should I believe what you say, Mr Koornhof?'

The Dutchman reached inside his jacket and brought out a sealed envelope which he waved in the air. 'Which of you,' he asked, somewhat unnecessarily, 'is Mr Bewdley?'

'That's me,' Bewdley said. He lifted his bowler hat.

'Then I have this despatch for you. Please open it. You will see that it comes from Major Douglas Haig of General French's staff –'

Halfhyde interrupted. He remembered that aboard the train the infantry officers had discussed Douglas Haig. 'The Cavalry Division? So far as I'm aware, they're not in this theatre of the war?'

Koornhof said, 'Major Haig has fingers in many pies, Lieutenant Halfhyde. Is that not so, Mr Bewdley?'

'Yes, I believe it is, Mr Koornhof.' The little man tore open the envelope; he read the message, raised his eyebrows a little, and handed it to Halfhyde. It was a handwritten scrawl, signed Douglas Haig, Staff Major, Cavalry Division. At the top, the address read Chieveley Station. The message indicated that the originally promised infantry escort was being withdrawn and that Bewdley was to proceed with an escort to be provided from the wrecked armoured train and to follow the instructions of the bearer of the message, Mr Klaus Koornhof, diamond merchant from Amsterdam, who would guide him and his consignment to Mr Jan van Buren.

Halfhyde caught Bewdley's eye. 'Genuine?' he asked. 'Are

you familiar with Major Haig's handwriting?'

Bewdley nodded. 'Yes, as it happens I am. The hand is his, Lieutenant Halfhyde, you may be sure.'

'Then I suppose we must obey.' Thoughtfully, Halfhyde tapped the envelope aganst his chin then looked up at the rider. 'This message puts me in your hands, Mr Koornhof. Are you to guide us all the way to the Drakensberg? If you are, then have you considered the commissariat? We expected only to march to Chieveley in the first instance; we have insufficient provisions and water for a long trek.'

'The trek will not be as far as the Drakensberg, Lieutenant. That also has changed. It is considered too risky –'

'That doesn't surprise me! Where to, then?'

Koornhof said, 'Another place. That is all I am authorized to tell you for now. I am sorry.'

Halfhyde flushed. 'I'm damned if I'll accept that, Mr Koornhof! It seems to me there is too little trust around. I must know where I am to march my seamen. It's not my custom to navigate blind at sea – or on land either. Before I take my seamen further, I demand to be put in full possession of the facts, Mr Koornhof. And that remark is also addressed to you, Mr Bewdley.'

Bewdley mopped sweat from his face and said, 'Oh dear. I thought you understood –'

'I understand nothing except that I am not being trusted, and that's a situation that's going to change instantly.' Halfhyde was growing angrier by the second. 'I see it as totally pointless for me not to know where I'm going –'

'Secrecy is paramount,' Koornhof interrupted. 'If we are attacked by Boer commandos . . . well, we might have to face the loss of the consignment, of course. But not necessarily more than that.' He paused, as if searching for words. 'What I mean, Lieutenant, is this: the whereabouts of certain persons – the *destination* of the consignment – these must never become known even if the consignment itself is lost. If the Boers take prisoners, those prisoners could be made to talk. It's essential that the right hand does not know what the left hand is doing. Surely

43

you must understand that? Certain persons are risking everything in the British interest –'

'And the commercial interest?'

Koornhof's face tightened. 'I do not understand.'

'Major Haig's message refers to you as a diamond merchant,
Mr Koornhof. I see a financial side to all this.'

'I think you are offensive, Lieutenant Halfhyde. That I
resent. Even merchants can possess patriotism –'

'Towards the British?'

Koornhof was holding his temper with difficulty. His face
darkening like Halfhyde's, he said, 'There are many angles.
There is an involvement of politics. I can say no more than that.
Mr Bewdley, I believe, understands very well.'

'Yes indeed,' Bewdley said in much agitation. 'He's right,
Lieutenant Halfhyde. He's right. Do please believe that. This
all needs very careful handling. You'll see that when we get to –
wherever it is we're going. And I don't know that any more
than you do. Not now.'

Halfhyde blew out a long breath and spoke again to the
Dutchman. 'And you, Mr Koornhof? If an attack comes, and
the Boers take you prisoner – are you so certain of remaining
silent under pressure?'

Koornhof smiled. 'No, I'm not. No man can be sure. But I
shall not be taken prisoner, Lieutenant Halfhyde.' He reached
into a saddle holster and brought out a heavy revolver. 'All the
time one bullet will remain in the chamber, one last one, for
myself. No, I shall not be taken.'

Halfhyde nodded slowly. Despite his feelings, he was
impressed. Any man who could coldly contemplate turning his
revolver upon himself must have a very strong motive, a very
strong urge to something or other – politics, aid for the British
cause against what were in fact his own people – or a very great
deal of money. Which? No doubt all would be revealed in the
end. In the meantime, Halfhyde had no love for traitors. He
decided he would stand his ground and the devil take this
Major Douglas Haig, and Bewdley of the Cape secretariat. He,
he said, commanded the naval escort and was responsible to

the Admiral commanding at the Cape. If he was given no
further information, he would march the consignment back to
the armoured train where it would be fully under the British
Army's control. On that he was adamant.

It was Koornhof who conceded defeat.

iii

Koornhof's story had startled Halfhyde; he didn't know
whether to believe it or not, but Bewdley had nodded at
everything the Dutchman had said, giving his tacit corrobora-
tion of the facts. The arrival of the gold bullion aboard the *Glen
Halladale* had been fortuitous. Its presence in Halfhyde's hold
had been reported ahead by the master of the steam transport
Tintagel Castle carrying troops from Southampton to the Cape,
troops whose assistance Halfhyde had requested by signal in
order to contain the break-out of convicts from his tween-deck;
and it fitted excellently into certain plans being formulated by
Major Haig. By the time the *Glen Halladale* had arrived at the
Cape, the disposal of the bullion, and of Halfhyde himself, had
already been decided.

Halfhyde had gone into a conclave with the Dutchman and
Mr Bewdley, out of earshot of the gunner's mate and the
seamen of the escort. Koornhof had confirmed straight out that
the basis of Haig's plan was bribery. There was a Boer leader
whose name Koornhof would not yet disclose who was known
to be avaricious and not wholly committed to the war against
the British; his land was being ravaged by the fighting and he
was losing money, and previously he had prospered and had
been friendly with the British and the government at the Cape.
Feelers had been put out, and clandestine meetings had been
held. The Boer would co-operate; but there had been haggling
over his price. The coming arrival of the gold bullion had
settled that.

'What's he to do for it?' Halfhyde had asked.

'He's to assist in lifting the siege.'

'Of Ladysmith?'

'Yes. As no doubt you know, General Buller's operations for

45

the relief have not so far been successful and his armies in Natal are currently held upon the Tugela River by the Boers under Commandant Botha. Buller's wish is to force a crossing of the Tugela, outflanking Botha by making his crossing well to the west of Colenso towards the foothills of the Drakensberg below Spearman's Heights, which are occupied by Lord Dundonald's mounted brigade. He will then take a small mountain known as Spion Kop, and this will give him a clear march of some twenty miles of plain to Ladysmith – if the Boers are not there.'

'And your man – this bribable Boer, Mr Koornhof – where does he come in?'

Koornhof said, 'He's close to Louis Botha. He's said to have influence with him. He can sway Botha's decisions.'

'And see that Buller's let through?'

'Roughly that, yes. The Boer forces will be withdrawn eastwards.'

Halfhyde made no comment. It was dirty, but it was war. If the plan succeeded, many British lives might well be saved. That was the sensible way to look at it. It would be up to the renegade Boer to learn to live with himself afterwards. And Sir Redvers Buller? That was what stuck in Halfhyde's throat. Buller was known to be a straightforward officer, loved by his soldiers, brave as a lion and never one to shrink from a battle. He surely wouldn't wish to win by such a subterfuge as this; it was at odds with his nature. Ever since the war had threatened, the newspapers back home in England had made much of Buller and his character. He was a British hero, cheered wherever he went. But Bewdley had said earlier that Buller had given his full approval. Now Koornhof confirmed this. Halfhyde was unable to argue; but his belief was that Buller had somehow or other had the wool pulled over his eyes.

He asked, 'And you, Mr Koornhof? What is your stake in this?'

Koornhof smiled. 'I am the broker, Lieutenant Halfhyde, but I assure you I am not fee'd.'

'But you have an interest.'

'Oh yes, I have an interest. As a Dutchman, even though the

Boers are Dutch and my government supports them, I can stand aloof and consider other matters.'

'Matters of trade?'

'Yes. I am a diamond merchant. Kimberley is important to me, for instance, and Kimberley like Ladysmith and Mafeking is currently under siege – there is no direct connection, of course, but if one siege is lifted by force of British arms, then others can follow fast –'

'The heart taken out of the Boers?'

Koornhof nodded. 'I wish the war to end.'

'In a British victory?'

'Yes. For this reason: I am convinced the British will win eventually in any case, and the faster the better, Lieutenant Halfhyde.'

Halfhyde said, 'Well, I can scarcely argue against that, of course.'

'Quite. I am glad you see that, however much you dislike the plan. You must also see something else: the identity of the Boer must never be revealed.'

Halfhyde gave a thin smile. 'I'd not like to be in his shoes if ever it was! Tell me something further, Mr Koornhof: how is this Boer to be trusted – trusted, in the event, to give Botha poor tactical advice, or in some way to impede his action against General Buller?'

'Because there's to be a hostage, Lieutenant Halfhyde. The son of the Boer leader has been delivered to the British, ostensibly taken as a prisoner of war, and he will be released – allowed to escape, that is – once Ladysmith is relieved. The matter is well covered.' Koornhof paused. 'Have I satisfied you?'

'You've satisfied my curiosity, Mr Koornhof. But not impressed me with your ethics.'

The Dutchman was good-humoured about that. 'I shall have to suffer your disapproval in that case. But you will now grant me the honour of your seamen as escort to the gold?'

'Where to, Mr Koornhof?'

Koornhof conceded once again. He said, 'Direct for the

Tugela, and General's Buller's camp.'

iv

Near the docks in Cape Town, in the filthy hovel's stench, the sound of wheels and hooves was heard outside and the man named Pieters left the room and went along the passage to the door. A covered wagon stood ready, with a bush-hatted Afrikaner holding the reins of two horses, and another man beside him. The driver lifted a hand in salute as Pieters was seen. Pieters said, 'Three minutes', and turned and went back inside. He glanced at Victoria Penn, standing white-faced in a corner of the room, her dress stiff with blood. He spoke to Mahon.

'The old woman. She will talk, my friend. She will talk of those who came and used her hovel. But she can't come with us, she is too smelly to lift into the wagon, and then to live with. And I doubt if she values her life overmuch.'

'So?'

'Well, she'll lose it in a good cause.' Pieters laughed. He brought out a revolver and looked at it, then put it back in its holster. 'Noisy. The knife is better.'

Victoria said suddenly, 'You said you didn't sanction beatings, and now you –'

'True. When such things are unnecessary. Now I am faced with a necessity.' Pieters turned to the Englishman. 'You, Mahon. Silence the girl. Quickly!'

Mahon moved fast and took Victoria in a hard grip, holding a hand over her mouth while Pieters drew a knife from his pocket and moved across for the old crone. Victoria shut her eyes tight. There was no more than a choking gurgle; but as she was pushed from the room she stumbled and opened her eyes involuntarily. The old woman had slumped sideways and her throat gaped open like a slit purse and welled with blood. Victoria was manhandled along the passage and into the back of the covered wagon. Mahon and his companions went in with her, and Mahon wound a piece of cloth around her mouth and fastened it tightly behind her head, while Flannery bound her

48

wrists together with rope. The horses were brought to life and movement by a jerk of the reins, and the wagon rumbled away in the opposite direction from the docks, making out of Cape Town. Half scared out of her wits, every lurch of the wagon painful, Victoria wondered why she hadn't been killed like the old crone . . . but, of course, the old woman was, or had been, just an anonymous native, a Kaffir of no account to anyone. If her own body had been found there would have been a hue and cry. She might die yet, once they were out into the veldt and her body could be hidden. Or there might be some use for her alive.

Meanwhile there was no escape. She was helpless; and at the mercy of Mahon and the other men, at least two of them convicts, on the run from both Dartmoor and the British Army. They would be desperate enough . . . .

The wagon left the outskirts of the town, heading in an easterly direction. Victoria's thought was that if the destination was Chieveley then it was going to take them a bloody long time to get there and maybe by the time they did Halfhyde would be out of harm's way.

FIVE

The distance to Buller's camp, Koornhof said, was not great, though somewhat farther than they would have had to trek to Chieveley. They marched on through the day's mounting heat, weary now, and hungry. They had brought at least some rations with them from the train and they had their water-bottles, though by this time there was little left of either. Koornhof said there was little likelihood of encountering any Boer detachment: they were now too close to the British positions and Buller's scouts would be active. Word had been sent through to Buller from Chieveley that the orders had been changed and the gold was being diverted to the Tugela, so it was possible they would even be met by a British patrol.

But the Dutchman was wrong.

Some half-hour after the order to march had been given, a dust-cloud rose ahead from above a low hill. Koornhof believed this would be a patrol of British mounted infantry; but Halfhyde ordered the stand-to nevertheless, and himself ducked down into the cover of some handy scrub and put a match to Major Haig's despatch, making sure that every scrap was burned. It was just as well he did: the riders were a ragged mob with bandoliers strung across black jackets or waistcoats or shirts, bearded men with bush hats. A quick count showed some forty of them. Halfhyde passed the word to open fire; but the situation was hopeless, the British heavily outnumbered. Some of the riders crashed headlong from their horses but the rest came on, firing as they charged the line. Four of Halfhyde's seamen fell and then the Boers had closed in, circling the small force and holding them helpless beneath the rifles. It was then that Halfhyde saw that Koornhof had taken a bullet through his throat and lay in a spreading pool of blood.

ii

From Cape Town the wagon had rumbled on through the night, stopping for brief periods to rest the horses. The two men in front took turns at driving; in the back Pieters and the two Englishmen took their turns at sleeping and keeping awake to watch Victoria. There was water and basic food in the wagon: bread, fruit and tins of corned beef. Victoria had gathered that their destination was indeed the vicinity of Chieveley and that the trek was expected to take around eight to ten days. Once they had cleared away from Cape Town and were out into open and desolate country, the gag had been removed and Victoria had started asking questions; but she got no helpful answers.

'Wait and see,' Pieters said. 'Do as you're told, that's all that's required of you.'

'Reckon I'm to be some sort of hostage, is that it, eh?'

'Perhaps.'

'It won't get you anywhere.'

'Halfhyde's –'

'I don't mean that much to him, mate. With him, it's duty first, all the bloody time it's duty first. You'll see!'

'We shall all see,' Pieters said with a grin. He wouldn't answer any more questions and he volunteered nothing. The trek went on and on; the monotony was appalling: trek, stop, eat, trek. The nights, when the horses were rested, were cold, the days a hot hell and beneath the canvas cover the air grew thick despite the open tail. The almost constant motion gave Victoria no respite; every lurch of the wagon was painful still. Her head ached and she felt sick from the movement, too sick to eat the corned beef, though she managed bread and water simply because she was determined to keep her strength up. She began to lose all hope, however; she would never see St Vincent Halfhyde again.

The naval party was marched off under guard. Before moving out the man in charge of the riders had dismounted and pulled the coverings off the handcart and looked in amazement at the bullion's dull gleam.

He stared at Halfhyde. 'What is this, then?' he asked.

'You've seen for yourself, have you not?'

'I see that it is gold bullion, yes. Where from, and to where does it go?'

Halfhyde said, 'Into Boer hands now, it seems.' He spoke indifferently; he had no feelings about the gold. It was part of an unpleasant deal and in a sense it served the authorities right that their plot had misfired. Bewdley on the other hand was in a terrible state of dither and anxiety and was almost in tears. He had failed to make delivery and had brought a complex scheme to nought; and his anxieties showed badly when the Boer pressed Halfhyde about the gold's purpose. But whatever his own feelings might be, Halfhyde had no intention of revealing anything to the enemy.

He said with a shrug, 'I've no idea. I have not been taken into the confidence of whoever ordered the movement of the stuff – I'm simply the officer of the escort, that's all.'

'As such, then, you must know the destination. You will tell me.'

There was little point in attempting to conceal the fairly obvious and Halfhyde said, 'The train was going to Chieveley – you know that. The gold was to be disembarked there.'

The Boer looked unconvinced but did not remark that the party was evidently not heading in the direction of Chieveley. He merely asked, 'And that is all you know?'

'That is all I know.'

'Or all you will say. In the meantime, I shall not linger to force answers from you. But it will be a different story when we reach our camp. Commandant Botha will wish to know more.'

'I'll be surprised,' Halfhyde said sourly, 'if he'll be inclined to question a gift horse too closely. I imagine he'll be satisfied enough with the bullion itself.' He glanced at Mr Bewdley: the little man was beside himself now. To be going to Louis Botha's camp with the gold intended to suborn Botha's own friend and comrade was a sorry trick of fate, but Halfhyde could see the funny side if Bewdley couldn't. However, he forebore to say so, to Bewdley's obvious relief. Bewdley had seen the glimmer in Halfhyde's eye and had feared the worst.

Halfhyde requested time to bury the dead; the Boer officer refused, leaving his own dead behind as well to be seared by the sun and pecked at by the birds of prey and any wandering animals. He repeated that he could not linger; as Koornhof had said, there might be British patrols. Koornhof's was the one body to receive special treatment: as a civilian with a British naval party, like Bewdley, Koornhof was of possible interest and his body might be recognized by Commandant Botha, so it was lifted and laid across the saddle of one of the riders. As the naval party was marched away under the Boer rifles, Halfhyde sent up a prayer that they might be intercepted by one of the British patrols, but the prayer was not answered. Not a solitary British soldier showed.

After a further hour's march the handcart reached the end of its endurance and sagged to total collapse, spilling the bullion out onto the iron-hard ground. The bars were distributed amongst the Boers' saddle-bags. The handcart was left, a sad heap in the scrub.

Another hour's ride and march in the blistering heat and then Halfhyde saw a township ahead, with a good deal of military activity going on, and what looked like ammunition dumps and a gun park. This would be Louis Botha's camp, no doubt the place from which he would make a final strike against besieged Ladysmith and its garrison, by this time surely brought to a low ebb. Halfhyde had been told aboard the train what the British troops in Ladysmith had been suffering: constant bombardment by the Boer artillery, and rations so low that they and the townspeople were reduced to eating rats. There was much sickness: dysentery was rife, as indeed it was amongst all the troops in the field, and more soldiers were dying of it than had fallen to the Boer marksmen.

They came into the town. From all sides men and women came out to watch the British naval prisoners being brought in surrounded by the Boer rifles. There was cheering, and fists were waved, but nothing more than that. The riders kept the crowds back and Halfhyde and his seamen were brought in safety to a small compound, otherwise empty, with a kind of bunkhouse at one end, with the perimeter surrounded by a high stockade fence topped with three separate layers of heavy barbed wire and with a high watch-tower overlooking it. As the prisoners were ridden in, two men were seen climbing the ladder to the platform, rifles slung from their shoulders. When the gate was secured, the Boer detachment rode away, taking the gold with them.

Halfhyde looked around. 'A grim enough place, Mr Bewdley.'

'To be sure it is.' Bewdley was literally wringing his hands, and his lips were trembling. 'Matters could scarcely be worse, Lieutenant Halfhyde, indeed they could not.'

'Keep your chin up, man! We're far from finished yet. Don't forget the gold.'

'Oh dear me, I'm not likely to do that!'

Halfhyde nodded. 'I suppose not. And it could prove our trump card – our only card in fact –'

'The gold must not be compromised,' Bewdley interrupted.

'Nonsense! It's compromised already, is it not? Now tell me this, Mr Bewdley: the highly-placed Boer that Koornhof spoke of – do you know who he is?'

Bewdley shook his head. 'No, I don't. Of course, I knew of his *existence*, since the whole scheme revolves around him. But his identity – no, I don't know that, Lieutenant Halfhyde. Apart from the principals, the *other* principals, the only name I know is van Buren who was to meet us at Chieveley.'

'I see. But let us do some hypothesizing, Mr Bewdley. Koornhof spoke of this man, this unknown Boer leader, as being close to Louis Botha. Close in spirit – but almost certainly close in a physical sense also. In short, he'll very likely be here

54

with Botha. Do you agree?'

'I dare say,' Bewdley said. 'Yes, I think that's likely.'

'In which case he'll be in a fair way to an attack of diarrhoea – I speak metaphorically – now that the gold has turned up in an unexpected way, and is in Botha's hands instead of his own.'

'Yes, that's very true.' Bewdley dabbed at his cheeks and fanned himself with the bowler hat. 'He'll be fearful of what we might divulge, though naturally –'

'Quite! So in a sense we have a friend at court. That's the hand we have to play, Mr Bewdley, and it will require care.'

'But what can we do about it?'

Halfhyde gave a laugh and laid a hand on the little man's shoulder. 'Why, as yet nothing, other than to co-ordinate the story you and I shall tell the Boers when they start their questioning. That apart, we wait, that's all. We display a masterly inactivity and we leave Louis Botha's traitorous friend to chew his finger-nails. Now, Mr Bewdley, make yourself comfortable inside the wooden hut that is to be our mess for so long as we're here, and think about our story. I shall be doing the same, and shortly we shall agree on what's to be said. In the meantime I shall make an inspection of the perimeter fence with Petty Officer Dunning.'

Bewdley looked alarmed. 'Oh dear me, Lieutenant Halfhyde, you're not thinking, are you, of an attempt to escape?'

'That depends,' Halfhyde answered, 'but a reconnaissance is a simple duty.'

Bewdley seemed about to say something further but thought better of it and turned away and went through the door into the hut. Halfhyde called to the gunner's mate and together they walked around the stockade. It was very secure, and rose some fifteen feet above their heads. The wood was smooth, giving no handholds or footholds, while even if there had been such any climber would have been held like a fly on flypaper by the barbed wire, a struggling target for the bullets of the guard in the watch-tower.

'Not a chance, sir,' Dunning said gloomily.

'Not at present,' Halfhyde agreed. 'But times may change.

Keep the men in good heart, Petty Officer Dunning. Tell them the sea's still in being, and it'll not be long before they're back upon it!'

Dunning nodded, but clearly didn't believe any of them would see the sea again until the war was over. Perhaps not even then; prisoners were always at the mercy of their captors' whims, and the Boer farmers were known to be hard men. Stories had circulated around the warships at the Cape that the Boers ate babies for breakfast and were more than capable of putting prisoners of war to the bayonet . . . .

They walked back together, watched closely by the men on guard, who had kept their rifles levelled on them all the time. The sun was high now, in its noon position, and had brought up the smells of the town – the poor sanitation, horse dung, animal carcasses on the plain. Flies buzzed and bit, and dust lay everywhere. Halfhyde suffered a sudden nostalgia for the sea, for the open deck of the *Glen Halladale*, rope and canvas straining as she flew before the westerlies of the Roaring Forties. By this time, the ship should have come round the Cape of Good Hope and be heading on a northerly course for Durban. She would not be all that far away once she had arrived in the port. Halfhyde spared a thought for Victoria Penn, a thought touched with more than a trace of irritation. She had complicated his life: the sea and women never mixed, they were far better kept apart. Many masters in the windjammers were accustomed to taking their wives to sea with them and in effect made their ships their homes. That would not suit Halfhyde. The seas were the place for men. A henpecked shipmaster would be a sorry sight . . . .

Nevertheless Victoria was by now a fact of his life. She had wormed herself in. He would be glad to see her again. He went to the bunkhouse to confer with Mr Bewdley as to their story.

iv

In the late afternoon an armed escort entered the compound and a Boer officer approached Halfhyde. He was required by Commandant Botha. Bewdley, it seemed, was not wanted yet.

56

Halfhyde could see the mounting strain in the little civilian's face, could see that Bewdley was apprehensive as to how far he, Halfhyde, would stick to the agreed story. Already he had issued dire warnings about what could and what could not be said. Questions could never be accurately forecast and there would have to be a degree of improvisation. Meanwhile there was an obvious reason for Halfhyde being interrogated alone: each would tell his own story separately, and afterwards Louis Botha and his advisers would compare the two.

Halfhyde was marched away between the four armed Boers, into the town itself, past the curious crowds staring at the British naval uniform, at Halfhyde's now stubble-covered face. He could feel the hostility: even the very dogs seemed to curl their lips and snarl. The British had come with their soldiers, their guns and their cavalry to disrupt the lives of peaceful farmers and townsfolk, to lose them lives and trade and property because of a dispute with Queen Victoria in far-off Windsor – that, no doubt, was how the Boers would be seeing it; and indeed, when Halfhyde was taken into what appeared to be the Town Hall and met Botha, flanked by bearded men who presumably were his staff, Botha started the conversation by saying something along these lines.

'I disagree, commandant,' Halfhyde said, standing between his guards. 'Your people – you know this very well – refused the British settlers their political rights whilst taxing them to the hilt – taxation without representation has led to war before this, in the American colonies –'

'This is our land, lieutenant. Our land!'

'Strictly speaking,' Halfhyde said evenly, 'it belongs to the Bantus. They were here first.'

Botha's face was cold with anger. He thumped a fist hard on the desk behind which he sat. 'We will not discuss the matter. You indulge in semantics. We shall talk instead about the gold.'

'Which you have stolen.'

'Semantics again. In war there is no stealing. There is seizure, which is different, and the gold is now subject to seizure. The booty of war, of the British intransigence that has

57

led to war. Now you will tell me what so much gold was doing in the middle of the veldt.'

Halfhyde said, 'I've already told your man all I know. The gold was to be delivered to Chieveley. After that, it would have passed out of my control and my knowledge.'

Botha said harshly, 'When apprehended you were not marching for Chieveley. According to the report from the men who picked you up, you were marching towards the British lines along the Tugela.'

Halfhyde shrugged. 'Poor navigation, commandant. I had lost myself.' He glanced at the faces of the men standing on either side of Louis Botha. Was one of them the man of whom Koornhof had spoken? It was possible; but none of them was showing any of the anxiety Halfhyde would have expected from a man whose traitorous activities could for all he knew be about to face exposure.

As though he had read some of Halfhyde's thoughts Botha said suddenly, 'And the man brought in dead, the Dutchman.'

'How do you know he was Dutch?'

Halfhyde thought it unlikely that Koornhof would have carried any papers speaking for his identity; and this appeared to have been the case. Botha spoke of articles of clothing from Amsterdam, of a Dutch appearance. He knew a Hollander when he saw one, he said.

'Good friends of yours, Commandant Botha.'

'Certainly. They are our people. Why was one of them with you, lieutenant?'

'I can't answer that.'

'Why not?'

Halfhyde smiled into the angry face. 'Because I don't know the answer. That is to say, I don't know what he was doing in the middle of the veldt. Naturally I asked questions, but I got no answers. He appeared from nowhere, from some scrub. He was hungry and thirsty. I took him on with my party.'

'To the camp of General Buller?'

'No. I told you, commandant, we were heading for Chieveley.'

'Yes, you told me that, I know. With the gold.'

'With the gold – yes.'

'I believe there is a connection between the gold and the Dutchman.'

Halfhyde shrugged, as much as to say, believe what you will, your beliefs are your own affair.

Botha said menacingly, 'You will tell me of the connection, lieutenant. You will tell me all the facts or there will be difficulties for you. I remind you, you are a prisoner of war. I remind you also, not all Boer prisoners in British hands have been well treated. There can be tits for tats.'

Halfhyde suppressed a smile: however excellent Louis Botha's English might be, he was not fully conversant with all the idioms of the language. Then it came to Halfhyde that he might play along a little way with the commandant and at the same time let the traitor know – if he was there present with his friend Louis Botha – that he, Halfhyde, had in fact a card or two up his sleeve. Something might well be precipitated thereby.

Addressing Botha again, he said, 'You ask for the facts, commandant. I'm very far from being in possession of them all. One thing, however, I can tell you for what it's worth.'

'Yes?'

'The Dutchman. He told me his name. That name was Koornhof.'

As he spoke the name, Halfhyde swept his glance around the men at Botha's side, a meaning look that he hoped might not be lost upon one of them. The man on Botha's right gave a small start and looked away from Halfhyde's eye. Halfhyde felt he might have scored a bull's eye. The man could be presumed to have seen Koornhof's body by this time, so that would be no surprise. But that man hadn't liked Halfhyde's stare and could well have taken the meaning in. But time would tell. Meanwhile Botha was pressing for more facts; but Halfhyde had nothing more to say for the time being.

Botha stood up. He said, 'Very well. You will not tell me and I do not believe you when you say you do not know. Valuable consignments of gold bullion do not travel about the veldt in the charge of someone who has no orders and no knowledge of what is to happen. You take me for an idiot, lieutenant. You will be taught differently. You will be held in solitary confinement, and on a diet of bread and water only, until you decide to speak.'

Botha strode from the room, followed by his staff. Halfhyde was taken by his escort and marched out, down the steps and out once again into the open. Shadows were being cast by the buildings and the day's heat was less, though there was an overall sultriness and some heat beat back from the walls of the houses and municipal buildings. Dogs yapped at the heels of the escort and were kicked away. As before, Halfhyde felt the enmity from the people in the streets as he was marched along. The British, the Uitlanders as they were called, had come unbidden to their land, had formed their own enclaves, had disliked the Dutch law and the Dutch way of doing things, and had, as was the way with the British, decided to throw their weight about and bring the British way to South Africa whether the Boer communities liked it or not. As a result they were getting a bloody nose. Halfhyde sensed the feeling of victory in the air. Kimberley, Mafeking and Ladysmith, all under siege despite the immense power of imperial Britain. And there was no doubt about it, General Buller was taking an unconscionably long while to lift the siege of Ladysmith. He was said to have a massive force that had fought bravely through to the Tugela River but for some reason it seemed he was holding them back from the final assault.

Could that reason be, simply, the gold? Buller was a humane man who disliked unnecessary losses of his soldiers. But for now that gold was gone so far as Buller was concerned and he might be forced to move on Ladysmith and commit his troops. But before he did that he might decide to investigate the non-arrival of the gold. In that, however, Halfhyde found small comfort: the gold was a needle in a haystack now to the British command.

The march was a long one, to the other side of the town from the compound where the rest of the party was being held. Halfhyde wondered about Bewdley, who would no doubt be

60

sent for by Botha. Would the little man break? Somehow Halfhyde didn't believe he would. He was so well aware of the importance of his mission, so well aware that this was his big opportunity in a personal sense; and his loyalty was beyond question.

The march ended at what looked like the town gaol, a grim, single-storey building with small, barred windows, and an exercise compound surrounded by a high brick wall topped with spikes and broken glass. Halfhyde was marched in and his details were checked by a man in uniform and then he was taken through a heavy door and down a steep flight of stone steps into a cellar. There were three doors leading off a passage-way; all stood open. There were evidently no other persons undergoing solitary confinement. Halfhyde was thrust into the middle cell and the door was locked behind him with a sound like the very knell of doom; then bolts were shot across and the escort went away.

After that there was total silence, and complete dark. No window apparently, nothing high up above ground level. The cell smelled dank and the air was heavy almost to the point of suffocation.

Halfhyde took a deep breath with difficulty: it was like breathing through a blanket. He felt around: the place was little more than four feet square. There was no bed, no chair – nothing beyond a stinking metal bucket over which he tripped and banged his head on the wall. He swore savagely. This was no place for a seaman. He felt the door all over, found a spyhole a little above the central point. He pushed a finger through: there was no escutcheon over the hole and no light beyond. But there was air. Indeed the spyhole was virtually the only source of air. Halfhyde bent to draw in all of it he could while the sweat began to pour from his body.

v

Mr Bewdley had been sent for by Louis Botha. He stood up to the Boer leader admirably. He gave nothing away. He knew what Lieutenant Halfhyde wanted: co-operation from a frightened man, a frightened traitor, a friend of Botha who, if discovered, must certainly face death.

'I know nothing,' Mr Bewdley said, quaking and holding his bowler hat close to the front of his body, like a shield. 'I'm very sorry but I really can't help, commandant. Like Lieutenant Halfhyde, all I was told was Chieveley.'

'But you are a civilian —'

'Oh, yes, indeed —'

'— from the Government at the Cape.'

'Yes.'

'Then you *must* know.'

Mr Bewdley shook his head. 'No, commandant. I'm not all that highly placed, you see.'

'What is your function?'

Mr Bewdley knew he must lie. 'Just a clerk, that's all.'

'But why send a clerk with a naval party commanded by an officer?'

'To keep a check, a count of the boxes —'

'A tallyman?'

'Just so, commandant, a tallyman.'

Botha nodded and then went off at a tangent. 'Tell me, Mr Bewdley, what do you know of the course of the war to date?'

'No more than anyone else,' Bewdley said.

'But you know it is not going well for the British.'

'I don't know any such thing,' Mr Bewdley said patriotically. 'General Buller will no doubt soon be marching upon Ladysmith, for one thing, and — and there've been *any number* of British successes — any number!'

'Small ones only.'

'Well, localized, perhaps,' Bewdley conceded.

'Yes. Yet the British Empire is vast and has very many soldiers and famous regiments. Britain is accustomed to fighting in the past, and has held India in check for many years. And we are only farmers, with neither taste nor aptitude for war. The British expected immediate victory, and have now had to bring in all the Empire to their assistance — and still there is no victory. Why have you not beaten us to our knees, Mr

62

Bewdley? Do you know the answer to that question?'

'Well, no. No, I don't.'

'But you are surprised?'

'Oh yes, very surprised indeed, I must say.'

'I offer you one good reason, one over-riding reason for our success: we know our land, Mr Bewdley, while the British do not. They are lost in the veldt. Our land is not Aldershot, not a parade ground, neither is it the North-West Frontier of India. The British are out of their element. Also, too much time has passed since the war in the Crimea and your officers have grown lazy and torpid and show a lack of professionalism – which was demonstrated at the Modder River when Lord Methuen got himself into such a position on the open plain that he was able neither to advance nor to retire – and then subsequently at Magersfontein sent his highland brigade to be mown down in darkness.'

Bewdley hung his head; it was true, and he was mortified. But he rallied and lifted his eyes sternly towards Commandant Botha. 'I don't see,' he said, 'what all this has to do with the gold.'

'You do not, Mr Bewdley?'

'Not in the least, Commandant Botha. Not in the very least.'

Botha said, 'If the British cannot win by force of arms they turn to other methods. They try to suborn their enemies. It was done in India on a massive scale, though not always with money. Decorations, honours for the maharajahs, all vain men. But here perhaps it is gold. What do you say to that, Mr Bewdley?'

'Goodness gracious me, commandant, are you suggesting an attempt at bribery?' Mr Bewdley's eyebrows went up convincingly.

'Yes. It will not succeed, of course – *would* not have succeeded. We Boers are not susceptible . . . but if any were, then they would pay with their lives when they were forced into the open. A stupid ploy, but I believe my assessment of the gold's purpose to be correct.'

'Well, I never!'

Bewdley was showing quite genuine shock. Louis Botha had arrived very quickly at the truth, and it was a truth that he, Bewdley, was going to find hard to deny. Whyever else, indeed, should gold bullion be discovered being pushed in a cart towards what might be considered the perimeter of Ladysmith? Nevertheless, Bewdley remained firm and said once again, 'Well, I never. What a suggestion, commandant! That is most certainly not the way we ever do things in the Empire, and I equally dispute what you just said about India –'

'You may dispute what you will, Mr Bewdley, but only inside your own head. The inside of *my* head is quite clear on the gold, and you are going to assist me in establishing my views as fact –'

'Me, how?'

Botha smiled; it was an unpleasant and threatening smile. 'I have friends in Cape Town, Mr Bewdley, men who have other friends with government contacts. I believe your name may be known in the secretariat as more than a lowly clerk, a simple nomadic tallyman – and this I shall find out, and then other enquiries will be made, using your name . . . . I think perhaps you understand?'

Mr Bewdley swallowed. He understood very well: Louis Botha might obtain the name of the Boer to be bribed, and if he did that then Lieutenant Halfhyde's scheme would most certainly go awry. Time might be short – Botha would have access to the telegraph – and the traitor in his camp might decide to get out while the going was good, that was to say, at once. With him would go the naval party's and Bewdley's last hope of regaining their freedom. And Lieutenant Halfhyde, of course, would know none of this.

What could be done?

There were always delaying tactics, if only his mind hadn't become half paralysed, leaving him unable to think properly. Some false leads, misinformation . . . but if Botha meant to invoke his friends with government contacts it was quite likely that misinformation would be quickly bowled out for what it was and then retribution would be made against the man on the spot – himself, Assistant Deputy Principal Horace Bewdley of the Cape secretariat. Oh yes, his name was known all right! Assistant deputy principals didn't grow on trees, after all; and once he had shaken the hand of His Excellency the Governor of Cape Colony, something never to be forgotten, something to be remembered with pride now, in his moment of danger, the moment when much depended upon him.

Mr Bewdley decided the best thing to do would be to play the coward. He thought it vital, over-riding, that Botha should be prevented from making contact with his friends at the Cape: Lieutenant Halfhyde had to be given time and the traitor had to be lulled so that he did not take flight. Everything depended on that traitor believing that it was the British party itself that meant danger to him. Mr Bewdley knew he had to cover that point as well, though at the moment he had not the remotest idea how he was to achieve that if he was also to convince Botha that the gold was harmless . . . .

Mr Bewdley coughed and said, 'Well, now, perhaps I *can* help, commandant. I don't know, mind. But it does seem a lot of bother. First I have to ask this: what's in it for me?'

Botha laughed, but there was scorn in his face. 'Every man has his price, Mr Bewdley. But your price is in my hands to be decided.'

'I don't ask for money.' Mr Bewdley's head was bowed, he couldn't meet Louis Botha's eyes even though he was acting wholly in the British interest. 'Just safety. Just freedom. I want to get back to Cape Town, commandant.'

'Then perhaps you shall do so. Say what you have to say, and then I shall decide.'

'I'd like to know where I stand first.' Bewdley began to shake; it was not entirely put on. His bowels felt loose and a feeling of sickness rose in him and he believed he might even faint with the strain of deception and the awful feeling that he was being looked upon as a traitor to his country in time of war. There was another aspect as well, and a very serious one: he had no idea in all the world what he was going to say Louis Botha. He muttered a desperate prayer that he might be sent inspiration.

'What are you saying, Mr Bewdley?' Botha asked.

'I – I'm communing with God.'

Botha nodded. 'That seems a good idea and one to be commended,' he said.

Mr Bewdley felt worse than ever; those who were about to die communed with God.

SIX

The wagon lumbered on; the days passed. Out in the South African tablelands the guard on Victoria grew slack: there was nowhere for her to run to, no escape. The country was bleak, and hot, and largely waterless. Food and water were strictly rationed by Pieters, and the supplies were added to whenever possible. There was the occasional water hole, used by the wild animals of the karroo and thus risky for human consumption except in a last resort, but as a precaution against an emergency Pieters had the empty water-bottles filled while the horses were watered. Wild fruit and berries could be picked now and again. The journey was taking longer than they had expected: there were many deviations around the wilder mountains and when the track grew steep the horses made heavy weather of it, and everyone, Victoria included, had to get out and push the wagon from behind.

Victoria grew more and more morose. She had had to fight off the attentions of the man Flannery, an easy enough thing to do once she had laid his cheek open with her finger-nails. Pieters had halted the wagon, come round to the tailboard, ordered Flannery out and given him a punch in the face that sent him staggering.

'There'll be none of that. There's too much at stake. Now get back in the wagon.'

Flannery had been docile after that: Pieters was a dangerous man to cross. But when the wagon was moving again Victoria called through to Pieters sitting alongside the driver.

67

'What's at stake now, eh? You won't find Captain Halfhyde now, mate! He'll have gone through bloody Chieveley by this time and rejoined the ship in bloody Durban.'

Pieters looked round. 'Perhaps,' he said. That was all; it wasn't the first time Victoria had made the point and he hadn't seemed anything but indifferent, not in the least worried. To Victoria, that spoke of Halfhyde and the gold being not Pieters' only concern; there was something else. What? She had not the remotest notion. There was no point even in trying to see the wood for the trees. The time passed slowly; another night came down, another halt, another rest for the horses after they had been watered at a water-hole.

Move on again with the dawn: there seemed to be no end as the horses plodded north-eastwards towards the Orange River and Natal. They passed by native villages from time to time and aroused curiosity from the Kaffirs, from whom food was bought. Pieters made enquiries about any fighting in the vicinity. There had been none, it seemed. They were not yet into the war zone, and the Kaffirs had been disturbed by neither British nor Boers. The bush telegraph had brought the villagers word that the British General Buller was massing his armies to the north, on the banks of the Tugela, and that the Boers still besieged Ladysmith. Victoria prayed that as they went farther north they would run into a British force. As to that possibility, she had had her orders from Pieters, who was in possession of apparently authentically-stamped documents giving him the authority of the British Commander-in-Chief to provide an ambulance wagon for use by the army in Natal. He was to be accorded free passage and, if he should require it, an escort. The woman he would say was a nursing auxiliary keen to get to the war zone: cleaned up now and with a new dress bought at a village *en route*, she would pass as such easily enough. If Victoria denied her role, or acted up in any way, then matters would go badly for Captain Halfhyde.

'How's that?' she'd asked sarcastically. 'You'll never get your hands on him, so –'

'Don't underestimate me. That would be a mistake.'

68

Bluff? Most probably; but there was something about Pieters that carried authority and Victoria was to some extent convinced. She would never bring harm to St Vincent Halfhyde whatever the risk to herself. So, playing safe, she would go along with Pieters' story; but there might be ways in which she could indirectly warn any British soldiers that Pieters wasn't what he purported to be. She asked what would happen if they were picked up by a Boer commando. Pieters answered that that was unlikely; the Boer commandos were operating mainly in the Transvaal and Orange River Colony; but if they were unlucky, he was at least a Dutchman and would be able to talk his way through. Victoria reckoned he would; Dutch to the Boers, British to the British – his name was spelt Peters on his forged documentation and she herself had taken him for English in the first place. And the Boers wouldn't interfere with a Dutchman risking his neck against the British in fulfilling family loyalties by travelling north to a sister in Estcourt the other side of the Drakensberg . . . .

ii

Halfhyde had no means of telling the time, whether it was day or night. His watch had been removed from his pocket along with all other possessions, and his boots had also been taken. Not a glimmer of light showed anywhere except when, at long spaced intervals, he was fed. At those times armed men came with a lantern, the cell door was opened, and a tray was pushed through by a foot. Bread and water only, as promised by Commandant Botha. This had to be taken in darkness relieved only by the lantern's light coming through the spyhole; the guards remained outside the door while he ate and drank. He was allowed five minutes and then the tray was removed, the men went away and total darkness returned. A feeling of claustrophobia came to him, almost a sense of panic that had to be fought down firmly. Sweat poured, his hands clenched into fists, he beat at his temples. He could rot in this stinking cell. What was happening to his seamen? What was Bewdley telling Botha? Was Buller reacting to the non-arrival of the gold? And

69

where, in truth, had the Dutchman Koornhof fitted, and van Buren who was supposed to have taken delivery of the bullion at Chieveley?

The conundrums whirled in his mind and made no sense. He began to think he was going mad, that all this was some fearsome dream, that he would wake and find himself aboard the *Glen Halladale*, in the sea's good fresh air and sanity, surfacing perhaps from a last night ashore with Edwards . . . .

But it was no dream, and when he did find sleep, and was woken from it, it was a bearded Boer who stood before him with a heavy revolver in his hand.

iii

God had sent no inspiration to Mr Bewdley: he was mute. He pulled out a handkerchief and mopped streaming sweat from his face. What could he say? Commandant Botha was waiting for the promised help, and was obviously growing impatient.

'Come, Mr Bewdley. I am a reasonable man. Tell me what it is you have to say.'

'Yes.'

'And then I shall see what I can do for you. You wish to go back to Cape Town. Perhaps you can. You are not a soldier.'

'No. No, indeed.'

'You have a wife, a family?'

'No. I'm a single man, always have been.' Mr Bewdley paused, continuing to sweat and then began to gabble. 'You might say I'm wedded to my work, Commandant Botha. My old father, he used to say, who travels alone travels the fastest. Or was it the other way round? Yes, come to think of it, it was.' He stopped; Louis Botha was looking more than impatient. 'Sorry, I'm sure.'

'So you are not to be a help, Mr Bewdley?'

'On second thoughts, I don't believe what I thought of saying is very important, commandant –'

'I shall be the judge of that.'

'Yes, well.' Mr Bewdley fiddled desperately with his bowler hat, as though it might speak to him in place of God. Then, as if

70

by a miracle, inspiration came and Mr Bewdley seized upon it. 'The gold. You were asking about that, of course.'

'Yes?'

'Well, I think – mind, I'm very far from certain, very far, but I *think* it was destined for Ladysmith. General Buller was to take it with him when he advances to the relief of the town, commandant. I wasn't told this officially, I wasn't told anything, but from certain observations this is what I deduce. Because it's so uncertain I thought, well, I wouldn't bother you with it after all, you see.'

'To Ladysmith for what purpose, Mr Bewdley?'

'Well, of course I don't rightly know, but I believe it's – it's by way of – of compensation to the townspeople.'

'British gold, Mr Bewdley, to be given to the townspeople?'

'Well, by way of the authorities. Not the actual *people* as such. But it comes to the same thing in the end. Rebuilding and so on. Making the town decent again, clearing up all the mess. A costly business to my way of thinking. A hundred thouand pounds sterling – a lot of money certainly, but –'

'But if that was what it was for, Mr Bewdley, I believe you would have been told. There would be no point at all in such secrecy as to the gold's destination, that is to say its ultimate purpose. I can understand the need for secrecy whilst *en route*, but the rest of it, no. You are telling me lies, Mr Bewdley. You are concealing the facts.'

'I'm not obliged to talk to you at all, commandant,' Bewdley said. 'I've been brought here against my will, captured and –'

'We are at war, Mr Bewdley, and you are a prisoner. You would do well to consider your position.'

Bewdley was in a quandary and approaching a state not far off panic. He had in fact made a tactical error now: whether or not Botha believed him, he might well have set the mind of the Boer traitor, the acceptor of British bribes, at rest. That man, if he was present, and Mr Bewdley believed he was since he was Louis Botha's friend and in the high command, might now believe the British escort to the gold genuinely did not know of its purpose. This was the precise opposite of what Bewdley had hoped to convey. He had muffed it badly. The traitor might well regret the loss of the gold, but much more, of course, of his son; but as to his own safety he would breathe easy and would be of no help to Lieutenant Halfhyde and his party. Mr Bewdley wrung his hands around his bowler hat and said, 'Oh dear, oh dear, this is all a great worry, a great worry.'

Botha remained silent for a few moments, then conferred in a whisper with two of his aides. When the whispered conference was finished he said, 'Very well, Mr Bewdley, you will not help me, so you will go like Lieutenant Halfhyde into solitary confinement.'

iv

The man who woke Halfhyde wore crossed bandoliers, cartridge-filled, on his chest, over a black waistcoat and a soiled white shirt. In the light from the lantern which he carried he stared down at Halfhyde. Shadows chased across the bare, dirty walls of the cell, changing their shapes as the lantern flickered in a draught coming down from above to bring some welcome fresh air through the open door.

'Who are you?' Halfhyde asked from the corner where he lay, uncomfortably, on the floor's stone.

'My name does not matter, Lieutenant Halfhyde. Time is very short – you must listen. You know the purpose of the gold bullion you have brought. I have had private words with your companion, Mr Bewdley. He was questioned by Commandant Botha, who knew he was not telling the truth about the gold.' The man paused, then went on with emphasis, 'I also knew.'

Halfhyde heaved himself up. 'So you're the –'

'Yes. The truth must not come out, so much will be clear to you. Obviously it is within your power to secure your removal from solitary confinement by telling Botha the facts. I make no bones . . . I would be arrested by Louis Botha and shot, and your General Buller would receive no assistance. I do not believe you will do this because of your orders and your knowledge. However, I believe Louis Botha will force the facts from Bewdley, given time. He has spoken to me of a firing

72

squad, and already Mr Bewdley is much agitated as to his future. As for me, I cannot take the risk. And nor, I think, can General Buller.'

'Are you saying you're going to get us out of Botha's hands, is that it?'

The Boer nodded, his eyes reflecting the light from the lantern. His voice, kept low, was tense. 'Yes. There will be a way, never fear. I –'

'I'll not leave without my seamen. All of them. And the bullion, which it is my responsibility to –'

'Yes. The bullion goes with you, to General Buller's camp on the Tugela, where my son is held hostage, as you know.'

'How are you going to get us out, for God's sake?' To Halfhyde it sounded an impossible suggestion. The compound was guarded from the watch-tower; all the sentries would be alert; he himself was in a guarded cell block. 'The very fact of prisoners in the camp will ensure that everyone's keyed up!'

'You may leave that to me, Lieutenant Halfhyde. I carry full authority here and I am confident – you will see. Also, I am not alone. I shall leave you now. I shall return after dark.' He looked down at Halfhyde's stockinged feet. 'I shall bring a pair of boots.'

'Size eleven,' Halfhyde said. 'I thank you for your consideration and I'll be glad of your assistance – much as I deplore your moral standards.'

The Boer made no comment. He left the cell, securing the door behind him, and then Halfhyde heard his heavy footfalls going up the stone steps. Almost immediately after, there were sounds indicating that someone else was coming down and then Halfhyde heard Bewdley's protesting voice. He was, Bewdley said loudly, a civilian and no one had the right to treat him like this. Strong complaints would be lodged by the government of Cape Colony. There was laughter and then the slamming of the door of the next cell and the sound of a key in the lock and the drawing of bolts. The guards went away up the steps and then there was silence. But after a short interval the silence was broken by a scrabbling sound on the dividing wall

73

and then a tapping.

Halfhyde tapped back. He saw little point in it, but possibly Bewdley wished the reassurance of contact, however remote. There were more return taps and then the scrabbling started again. Some while after this there was a scraping sound and then Bewdley's muffled voice came through to him.

'Sorry if I'm startling you, Lieutenant Halfhyde. A loose brick. An earlier occupant, perhaps, whose handiwork was never discovered.'

'Perhaps.'

'Anyway, we can communicate now.'

'In whispers. No chances.'

'No, indeed. Has Commandant Steen spoken to you?'

'Someone has.'

'It'll have been Commandant Steen, our traitor, Lieutenant Halfhyde. He had words with me also. He carries weight with Botha as of course we know, and he told Botha he might be able to make me talk. I didn't, naturally —'

'But *he* did?'

'Yes,' came Bewdley's whispering voice. 'After that, well, I confirmed it all and we understood one another.'

'He believes Botha's likely to break you.'

'Yes, I did tell him I was nearing the end of my tether, Lieutenant Halfhyde, which I'm not and wouldn't ever give away my government's secrets, which I hope you realize?'

'Oh, certainly.'

'But I did deem it expedient to let Steen *think* I would. Do you think I did right, Lieutenant Halfhyde?'

'Very right indeed. You may be the means of getting us out, Mr Bewdley. I stress the "may". Frankly, I doubt if this Steen can bring it off.'

'Oh, I don't know; he seemed absolutely confident. And his life's at stake, you know.'

'Ours too,' Halfhyde said sourly, 'if we're caught trying to escape.'

'It's our duty to try to do that, as I understand naval and military matters.' Mr Bewdley gave a cough through the gap.

'Sorry I'm sure. That was presumptuous of me.'

'Not at all, Mr Bewdley.'

'You're very magnanimous, Lieutenant Halfhyde. Do you know what my old dad used to say?'

'No, what?'

'My old dad, he always said real gentlemen were magnanimous.'

'He did, did he?' Halfhyde forebore to ask if Bewdley senior would have considered the liner-bound gentry who had squashed him flat at Fenchurch Street Station as magnanimous. He whispered back through the hole in the wall that they should not tempt fate; conversation should now be restricted to necessities.

'Yes, well, of course you're right, Lieutenant Halfhyde, but it was nice to have a chat . . . .'

Halfhyde settled down for what might be a long wait. He still saw no prospect whatever of success and had no wish to see his seamen or himself cut to ribbons by the Boer rifles during the coming night. The whole thing would be hazardous in the extreme, even to the extent of being suicidal.

But, as Bewdley had said, he had a duty. And, for what it might be worth, Bewdley sounded very much happier. He was full of confidence. Undoubtedly Steen had impressed him with his ability to fulfil his promise.

SEVEN

Halfhyde spoke again, whispering through the hole to ask if Mr Bewdley had been given any idea of what Steen had in mind, how the escape was to be brought about.

Mr Bewdley had not. 'He was not forthcoming, Lieutenant Halfhyde, not forthcoming at all in that respect. But I've every confidence he'll manage it.' There was a pause. 'Do I take it the name's not familiar to you, Lieutenant Halfhyde?'

'You do. I've never heard of him.'

'He's well known to the Cape government, very well known. Indeed I did have my own suspicions that he was the one the gold was going to, since he's known to be a close personal friend of Commandant Botha and one of his leading field commanders. His influence with Botha must be very great. Also, he'll be obeyed without question by the ordinary Boers when he makes his arrangements for our escape.'

Halfhyde was still very far from convinced. Steen might well be obeyed at the time of giving his orders, but how was he going to square his position with Louis Botha afterwards? It was vital to the British plan that his standing with the Boer leader remained intact; Steen would be as aware of this as anyone else, naturally. With his own son in British hands he was really in an impossible position between the two sides and he would have to step with extreme care.

Time passed slowly in the total darkness of the cell. Halfhyde was alert to every sound that reached him, his ears straining. The sounds were few in fact, no more than an occasional movement of the prison guard above. In the next cell Bewdley remained silent. Halfhyde paced, a caged tiger, two steps one way, two the other. He cursed the land and its problems, its terrible constrictions when matters went awry. He longed for the freedom of the seas, the open water, the gales and calms, the light of sun or moon, the chasing clouds and the vitality of storms.

ii

Above the cells the moon was coming up now, a pale crescent spreading silver across the veldt, over the township, over Botha's military camp and the sentries in the watch-tower. The compound was deserted; the seamen, the gunners of the escort, were by now confined in the hut, where they lay in their narrow bunks on palliases, some wakeful, others managing to find sleep. Petty Officer Dunning was one who lay awake, staring at the bottom boards of the bunk above his head and thinking, like Halfhyde, of the sea and the heavy armoured cruiser from which he had come not so many days before. Dunning had little more idea than Halfhyde of the precise time but it could be about two bells in the first watch and aboard Her Majesty's Ship *Terrible* rounds might be in progress, the cruiser's commander stalking through the messdecks and flats behind the master-at-arms and his candle-lantern. Soon Pipe Down would be piped on the bosun's calls, the bosun's mates making their way about the ship to turn the hands into their hammocks, and the cruiser, apart from the striking of the bell at the proper intervals, would lie as silent as this miserable prison compound . . . .

Dunning stirred on his straw, wondered how long it would be before he rejoined. No doubt it would be as long as the war lasted, but surely a bunch of rustic hayseeds couldn't withstand the might of the British Army for much longer? Guns and horses and massed infantry, discipline and a long fighting tradition must soon tell. But the Boers were fighting for their own homeland on their own soil and that also could tell, as Dunning admitted to himself as he lay sleepless; and there was the disease, the terrible dysentery that seemed by all accounts not to affect the Boers while the British soldiers died in their hundreds, outrunning the capacity of the medical columns. The conditions in the field were said to be virtually unendurable. In a sense the naval party were the lucky ones; they had beds and food and they were safe from the guns.

And what would that Mr Halfhyde be doing? And the little man in the bowler hat and the once-starched collar and cuffs, a city clerk transmogrified into an attachment to a gun's crew in the South African veldt of all the unlikelihoods. And there was the gold bullion: in that there was much to intrigue a simple sailor. There was always the lure of gold. Men had fought and plundered for it, had been led from the paths of rectitude by it. Halfhyde and Bewdley could be up to anything for all he, Dunning, knew.

Dunning got out his bunk and went restlessly across to a barred window. Looking out he could see the watch-tower manned by the two sentries, their rifles clearly visible in the light of the moon, slung from their shoulders as they talked together and cast an occasional glance down into the empty compound.

Dunning's instinct was for a break-out. But the instinct could never be put into practice. They would all be mown down in minutes.

He was still looking through the bars when the hut seemed to lift into the air and fall back again. Away to the east a brilliant sheet of red flame appeared on the heels of a massive explosion that rocked the township and was followed by seemingly endless smaller explosions.

iii

Halfhyde and Bewdley, closer than Petty Officer Dunning to the explosion, had fancied their last moments had come. They seemed at first to be pressed into the ground, and then released as if upon springs. The wall between the two cells shed a few bricks and Halfhyde found himself thrown to the floor.

From next door Mr Bewdley, sounding out of breath, asked,

78

'Are you all right?'

'I think so.'

'So am I, praise God.'

'Listen,' Halfhyde said peremptorily. There were voices from overhead, where apparently the heavy door at the top of the stone steps had been broken open. Men were speaking in Dutch; Halfhyde was unable to follow but Bewdley whispered through the broken wall.

'One of them's Commandant Steen, I believe, Lieutenant Halfhyde.'

'Come for us, I assume. This is where the escape starts – with an explosion brought about by Steen. You may start praying, Mr Bewdley, if that's your inclination, for we're certainly going to stand much in need of the Almighty's help tonight!'

'Amen,' Mr Bewdley said, but said it more as an expected reaction than as a fervent supplication or hope. Halfhyde reflected that there was more in Mr Bewdley than he would have suspected; he had taken the explosion well and was in full control of himself. A moment later footsteps were heard descending and light glowed beyond the spyhole. Halfhyde looked through: there was a lantern held above the head of a man whom he recognized as his earlier visitor. Bewdley looked through the spyhole in the other door and whispered, 'Commandant Steen, Lieutenant Halfhyde.'

Halfhyde's door was unlocked. Accompanied by another man, Steen stood there with the lantern and a heavy revolver. He said, 'Lieutenant Halfhyde and Mr Bewdley, you will be moved to more secure quarters. You will make no attempt to escape. If you do, you will be shot.'

'What's going on?' Halfhyde asked. 'That explosion –'

'An ammunition dump. We suspect a traitor in the camp.' Steen's face was impassive, his tone even. 'Or perhaps British troops are closer than we thought, and there has been a sortie. Our men are ready. Now come. Commandant Botha wishes words with you again.'

Steen stood back, waiting for the two to emerge. His revolver covered them. Halfhyde and Bewdley came out, and were gestured to climb the steps behind Steen's companion. Steen brought up the rear, the muzzle of the revolver close behind Bewdley's spine. Reaching ground level they were joined by another armed guard. Through the gaol windows, now shattered with broken glass lying everywhere, flames could be seen reaching high into the night sky, brilliantly lighting Botha's camp. There was some talk between Steen and the prison guards, some obvious argument followed by resigned shrugs from the guards, and then they were leaving the gaol compound with Steen alone. Steen explained as they went along. 'I have told the guards I have your parole and will take you myself to Commandant Botha – every man, I said, is needed to fight the fire and maintain security, and the guards will be better employed in giving their assistance.'

'And us?'

'You will see. All you have to do is keep close to me.'

'My seamen –'

'Yes. You have my word.'

'So, I presume, had Louis Botha,' Halfhyde said. There was a sharp indrawn breath from Mr Bewdley, who saw this as an indiscretion, but Halfhyde cared nothing for that. 'I shall not leave the camp without my seamen –'

'You will not. They will be with you. You have more than my word to rely upon, Lieutenant Halfhyde. Remember General Buller has my son.'

They moved on into the town itself, Steen giving them their direction as he kept close behind them, still covering them with his revolver. Buildings were burning or shattered, men were running in all directions, orders were being shouted, and they remained unchallenged in the general panic. Steen was naturally known to everyone, his movements would never be brought into question. They moved, going fast now, right across the township until Halfhyde saw the prisoner of war compound ahead with the sentries manning the watch-tower. Here the light from the blazing ammunition dump was more muted, and the compound itself was in the shadow of a big storehouse that stood between it and the fire. Steen pushed Halfhyde and

Bewdley ahead of his revolver until he was within shouting distance of the watch-tower; then he halted and called out to the sentries.

'This is Commandant Steen. I have orders from Commandant Botha. You will come down, both of you, and bring out the prisoners. Quickly now – there is no time to be lost.'

The men obeyed, coming fast down the ladder and approaching Steen from around the barbed-wire-topped stockade. The Boer leader spoke to them in Dutch; they turned away to enter the compound and approach the hut where the seamen were being held. By this time the man on night guard of the hut itself had appeared and had had words with Steen, and he turned away with the sentries from the watch-tower, a hand on the keys chained to his leather belt. Halfhyde was taken aback with the speed and treachery of the Boer's next move. Steen had brought out a second revolver which Halfhyde recognized as British Army pattern. He fired fast, three shots in rapid succession, and all well aimed. The guards went down flat; Steen stepped forward, fired three more rounds, one into each man's head, then bent to remove the prison keys from the belt and handed them to Halfhyde.

He said, 'Lose no time, Lieutenant Halfhyde. You may not like this, but I have kept my word. Bring out your men, and muster them in the shadows by the warehouse. If you are very fast, nothing will be seen, since all the activity is on the other side of the town. And now you will take one of my revolvers – *this* one.'

He thrust the British Army revolver into Halfhyde's hand. The act instantly galvanized Halfhyde into action: he had stood appalled, shocked by what the Boer had done. But if he should be taken now, with British bullets in the dead guards' bodies, he was as good as dead himself.

iv

'A dreadful experience.' Mr Bewdley mopped at his face, which was streaming sweat. He was shaking like a leaf by this time: never had he known such happenings. By now they were some four to five miles from the town by Halfhyde's reckoning, clear away and intact, all the seamen plus the bullion distributed in sacks borne by the men. The bars had been stowed away in a strong-room inside the warehouse, a strong-room to which Steen had held the key. This time using his original Boer revolver, he had shot down the unsuspecting guards. While the bullion was being brought out, Steen had had words privately with Halfhyde, telling him more of the facts of the gold's involvement. Then, with all the objectives achieved, he had instructed Halfhyde to fire a round into his leg and then to knock him unconscious with the butt of the revolver. This Halfhyde had done with a certain amount of satisfaction: the man was a murderer as well as a traitor. Halfhyde would have liked to shoot him dead; but he had to live, and he had to appear respectable in Louis Botha's eyes, a loyal Boer who had done his best to prevent the escape. No doubt he would get away with it.

Bewdley said, 'Will he not face questioning as to why he told the cell guards we were wanted by Commandant Botha, Lieutenant Halfhyde? He didn't shoot them, remember.'

'No. I asked him that. His answer was that we *were* wanted by Botha. He'd suggested to Botha that we should be brought out and questioned about the British positions, any likely patrols that might have penetrated.'

'And set off the explosions?'

'Exactly, Mr Bewdley.'

'I see.' Bewdley marched on, sounding out of breath as his short legs moved across the veldt. It was dark still and the moon had gone behind a range of hills. Steen had given Halfhyde his directions together with a pocket compass and he was not worried about missing the Tugela. It was unlikely, the Boer had said, that they would run into any hostile patrols – they were more likely to pick up a British one, since Sir Redvers Buller would be anxious to glean all possible information about the Boer dispositions and strength. Nevertheless, the possibility of Boer patrols did worry Halfhyde. His concern was the likely pursuit from Louis Botha's camp once the escape had become known. It would be fairly obvious which direction they would have taken. Steen had been firm that he would deflect any such pursuit, insisting to Botha that with General Buller poised to march upon Ladysmith's besiegers, it would be foolish in the extreme to risk the capture and interrogation of any of their men, who might be made to part with vital information about the Boer intentions. He had, however, taken the precaution of routeing Halfhyde well south in the first instance to avoid the direct route to the Tugela; this would mean a longer march but would give greater safety. In the meantime, if they were attacked, then they had the three rifles taken from the slaughtered strong-room guards plus the revolver given to Halfhyde by the Boer, who had been unable to lay hands on the seamen's own rifles and bayonets – they had been removed to the armoury in the first instance and then issued to those of the Boers who had no rifles of their own.

Bewdley said, 'I don't believe the plan is compromised in any way, Lieutenant Halfhyde.'

'A pity, for it's a dirty one and I would prefer to have had no part in it.'

Mr Bewdley found a suitable cliché: 'All's fair in love and war, they say.'

Halfhyde gave a snort. 'So far, this war has been a gentleman's war. There has been chivalry on both sides, and paroles have been respected. That will change when this night's events become known, as in time they must.'

'Only if we reveal them,' Bewdley said, 'which we must never do.'

'We're not the only ones concerned, Mr Bewdley –'

'No, but –'

'Whilst the gold was being brought out, I had an interesting conversation. The Boer traitor told me something which perhaps you do not know. The man who was killed earlier, Mr Bewdley, when we were picked up by the Boer patrol – Koornhof. It seems he was more involved in this business than appeared to be the case. More involved in a personal sense if you follow me.'

'I'm afraid I don't.'

'Then I shall tell you what Steen told me.' Halfhyde paused. 'Koornhof – this we know, since he told us – was a diamond merchant from Amsterdam, and it appears that he was a friend of Steen, a friend and a business associate of many years standing. He was to assist Steen in the handling of the gold, he and the man van Buren, who is currently waiting in Buller's camp for the delivery.'

'Assist him, Lieutenant Halfhyde?'

'Yes, Mr Bewdley. No traitor could hope to make any use of the bullion in South Africa, so much is obvious. Koornhof and van Buren were to take delivery of the consignment in the name of Steen, and arrange for its shipment to Amsterdam, where in due course Steen would take it over.'

Bewdley dabbed at his face. 'You mean Steen intends to leave the country?'

'Yes. He means to desert after he's done what he's being paid British gold to do. He'll take his reward in the comfort and safety of the Netherlands, Mr Bewdley.'

'Goodness gracious! I suppose that's only sensible in the circumstances. But I wonder why he told you all this, Lieutenant Halfhyde?'

Halfhyde said, 'Because of this van Buren, that's why. Koornhof being dead, it's now in the hands of van Buren, whom we have yet to meet –'

'But I still fail to see –'

'Steen does not wholly trust van Buren. Had Koornhof not been killed . . . But Steen believes van Buren's up to no good. That's it, in basis. This is news to you, Mr Bewdley?'

'Indeed it is!' Bewdley seemed thoroughly agitated. 'What are the grounds for this, Lieutenant Halfhyde, may I ask?'

Halfhyde shrugged. 'There was no time for more explanation than I was given. Steen was in a hurried situation and a dangerous one. Let us call it a strong suspicion on his part.'

'I should have been informed earlier –'

'Well, no matter now, Mr Bewdley. As things stand, Steen has urgently asked me to pass the information on to General

Buller and ask him to make alternative arrangements for the safety of the gold. In other words, not to entrust it to van Buren.'

'To whom, then?'

Halfhyde shrugged. 'That will be up to Buller. It's not our concern, Mr Bewdley. But if anything untoward should happen to the gold, then the co-operation of Commandant Steen may well be in some doubt. The only thing to hold him to his bargain would then be his son – and he knows that Sir Redvers Buller is an honourable man who in fact would see to it that the son was properly treated and his life preserved even though he's in Buller's camp as a hostage. In short, Steen would be prepared to take a chance as to his son if it should come to that.'

Mr Bewdley had nothing to say. He marched on in silence. Halfhyde grinned to himself. There was a certain amount of dudgeon in the atmosphere; offence had been taken. As the representative of the Cape secretariat, Mr Bewdley and not Halfhyde should have been entrusted with the new information. Halfhyde left the little man to his resentment and turned aside for a word with Petty Officer Dunning, who, like Halfhyde himself, was bearing his share of the bullion. The bars were heavy, weighing the men down on the march, and frequent rests were necessary. But reasonable progress was being made nevertheless, and there was no sign of any Boer pursuit: Steen was proving efficient in his manipulation of Louis Botha. By the time the dawn was in the sky and the first hint of the coming day's heat was felt, the naval party were, by Halfhyde's estimate, no more than a dozen or so miles from the Tugela. And some half-hour later, while the men were once again resting beneath the shade of some scrub, Dunning drew Halfhyde's attention to the southern horizon.

'Something moving, sir.' He pointed.

Halfhyde narrowed his eyes to look into the far distance. 'A covered wagon, I fancy,' he said.

The wagon moved closer behind the weary horses. Halfhyde had ordered his party to remain fallen out. He found nothing sinister in the fact of a covered wagon on the veldt; it could be a nomadic Boer family on the move from one township to another, though he was surprised that they should be moving north towards the war zone. In any event, if they were hostile, they would have the legs of his bullion-burdened seamen; and he preferred to wait in cover and see what developed. His party was unlikely to pass unnoticed, but his expectation was that when the occupants of the wagon recognized British uniforms they would sheer away and keep their distance.

In that, he was proved wrong.

From the wagon, as it came nearer, Pieters watched through a pair of field glasses, having picked up the group in the scrub with his naked eye. After a while he lowered the glasses and handed them to Flannery.

'Take a look,' he said.

Flannery adjusted the lenses and looked. He said in amazement, 'Well, I'll be damned! Sailors . . . no gun battery, but sailors!'

Pieters gave a quiet laugh. 'It's too much of a coincidence to be anyone but Halfhyde, I think. There cannot be two such parties. But we shall find out. Luck may be with us, my friend!'

EIGHT

For Victoria, the long ordeal in the lumbering wagon had become more and more nightmarish as day succeeded day in an apparently unending torture of heat and discomfort and fear. She lay inert in the back of the wagon, spiritless and defeated for the first time in a somewhat turbulent life, a life lived with courage and defiance. All defiance had gone now and the future seemed hopeless. She had gathered from scraps of overheard conversation that Pieters intended eventually to head east and go to ground with some associates in Natal and try to pick up some information that would lead him to the gold. And there had been mention of Durban and the *Glen Halladale.* Victoria had begun to gather something else as well: the men had never entertained any serious hope of intercepting Halfhyde before he handed the gold over. The gold would have reached Chieveley and would be beyond their grasp. But they were far from finished. What they talked of meant little to Victoria but she had heard mention of a man named Koornhof and another named van Buren, Dutchmen by the sound of it, and she believed that hopes were being entertained of something van Buren might be able to do. That was all. Victoria had listened only in case there was specific mention of St Vincent Halfhyde himself, which there had not been; she had become too listless to bother herself with any other considerations.

And then, suddenly this early morning before the wagon had turned further to the east, she had heard Halfhyde's name spoken and had taken in the fact that there was a naval party ahead of the wagon. Relief and happiness surged through her like a flame.

ii

Flannery was cautious: so was Mahon. Mahon said, 'They'll be armed for sure.'

'So are we,' Pieters pointed out. 'And I see no arms.' He had studied the distant group closely through his field glasses. 'It's curious, but it seems to be a fact.'

'Easy enough to hide them.'

'Easy, perhaps, but pointless, wouldn't you say? Anyone would expect weapons in the circumstances, and they wouldn't have any reason to hide them from a wagon.'

'So what do we do?'

Pieters said, 'First we gag the woman. See to that, Flannery.' Flannery scrambled through into the back of the wagon; Pieters lifted his glasses again, then after a while handed them to his companion. 'You'd recognize Captain Halfhyde. Take a look now. The one in officer's uniform.'

Mahon stared ahead, picking out the officer as he adjusted the lenses. After a moment he said, 'Yes, that's him all right.'

'You're sure?'

'Positive. Jesus, I saw the man often enough walking his poop aboard the *Glen Halladale* when we were brought up from the convict deck! I'm not likely to forget him, nor to be mistaken.'

Pieters nodded. 'A stroke of real luck, then. Almost incredible! In all the veldt . . .' He didn't finish the sentence. He began issuing his orders: the naval men would be approached, slowly and in apparent peace, the wagon ambling along without a care in the world but the guns ready to open fire beneath the canvas cover, when he, Pieters, gave the word. 'But not Halfhyde,' he said. 'I need him alive.'

The wagon moved on, closing the gap.

iii

'Coming straight for us, sir,' Petty Officer Dunning said.

88

Halfhyde shrugged. 'Ships that pass . . .'

'Sir?'

'We'll do no more than exchange greetings, I expect. On the other hand, they appear to be bound for the Tugela – it's odd enough certainly. Would you expect to find British families on the move, Dunning, perhaps for the safety of General Buller's camp?'

Dunning said doubtfully, 'Why, sir, I'm sure I don't know. This whole land's a mystery to me, sir . . . but they'd hardly be Boers, I reckon, not here, so close to our lines.'

'Quite. Well – we shall see. But it occurs to me they might provide some of us with handy transport, Dunning! The gold grows heavy, the more so each step once we move out again.'

'Aye, sir,' Dunning said with feeling. 'You'll commandeer the wagon, then, sir?'

'If necessary. First, I'll merely ask a favour.' Halfhyde's hand dropped to his revolver holster, provided along with the weapon itself by Commandant Steen. He would not be provocative; but the asking of favours might need a little backing. Now the wagon was little more than a quarter of a mile distant; and as it swayed closer Halfhyde saw a tall, slimly-built man holding the reins, dressed in a white shirt and dark trousers and wearing a bush hat. He could be either Briton or Boer; but there seemed to be no enmity. The man sat easily, and waved a hand in greeting.

Halfhyde waved back, waited until the wagon came closer, then called out.

'British, or Boer?'

'British. As I see you are.'

'Where are you bound?'

The man gestured towards the north. 'The Tugela.'

'For what purpose?'

'Why, I'm going home – to Natal. I've been on a business trip to the south. I sell – oh, all manner of things, some useful, some not –'

'An honest man, it seems! You're a general trader, then?'

'Yes. And you are a seafarer, out of his element.' There was a hint of amusement visible in the man's face as the wagon came on and then pulled up some ten yards short of Halfhyde's group. 'Do I understand you to be, shall I say, a little lost, lieutenant?'

'Not lost, no. But weary from a long march, and bound like you for the Tugela. If we could march with you and take turns to come aboard your wagon, we'd be very grateful.'

'Well, you'd be welcome enough, to be sure. But I think we should exchange identities, my dear sir. As for me, my name is Pieters.'

It could have been Peters or Pieters in Halfhyde's ears; but he found himself for no apparent reason with an almost imperceptible unease when he said, 'I am Lieutenant Halfhyde of the Naval Reserve –'

'A naval brigade, or part of one, without field guns?'

Halfhyde answered formally, 'I can't tell you any more than my name and rank, Mr Peters. I've no doubt you understand that.'

'Yes, of course, and I apologize for my impertinent question. But the situation in these parts is unclear, in a military sense, and I am bound as you now know for the Tugela, where General Buller is encamped. I'm sorry, but if you're to accompany me I think I must ask for formal identification in spite of the uniforms. You have papers, saying who you are?'

Halfhyde shook his head. 'I had, but have no longer. I fell in with some Boers . . . . It's a long story and one I can't relate.'

'I see.' The man seemed perturbed by this news but went on easily enough, 'Well, perhaps it's not important. But if you'd step up to the wagon, Lieutenant Halfhyde, we could have a mutually helpful talk.'

Halfhyde's vague unease had strengthened: the request was, he considered, a strange one. He said, 'We are talking now. I find that satisfactory enough. If you prefer not to be cluttered with my seamen, that's your affair. But I must remind you, I have the power, as any officer in the field in time of war has, to requisition you as necessary transport.'

There was a shrug from the man on the wagon's box and

Halfhyde saw him turn his head a little towards the covered back. At the same moment he noted a small movement of the canvas, a lifting of it away from the securing rope, and he believed he saw the dull gleam of gunmetal. He reacted on the instant, calling to Dunning to scatter the men and get them down on the ground, and ran himself direct for the wagon's driver, his revolver now out of its holster. He had gone no more than three paces when the guns opened from the back of the wagon, raking at close range into the startled seamen, riddling the bodies that had dropped to the ground, keeping up a continuous fire until the last twitches of life had been extinguished.

iv

As Halfhyde had gone forward, Pieters had been in difficulty with the horses. They had reared and whinnied but although Pieters had managed to bring them under control before they bolted, Halfhyde had run into flailing hooves and one of them had scraped the side of his head and laid him flat. When he came to it was all over; he was lying on the ground with his hands roped together behind his back and Pieters was still calming the horses. Halfhyde lifted his head and looked around at slaughter: Dunning and all the others lying still and dead, a bloody scene with the stench of gunsmoke still present. Beside himself one man had survived: Bewdley, dragged from behind the scrub by a man from the wagon, mute but with tears streaming down his cheeks, his face white as chalk and his limbs shaking so badly that when the man let him go he slumped to the ground helplessly.

Pieters came across to Halfhyde.

'Who's the civilian?' he asked.

'I have nothing to say.'

'Never mind, I'll be finding out. Where's the gold?'

'The gold?' Halfhyde stared into the man's eyes. 'What gold?'

A frown crossed Pieters' face. 'Don't try delaying tactics, lieutenant, or it'll go badly for you. You spoke of a Boer attack.

Don't tell me – they took it. I want to know where they went.'

'How should I know that?'

Pieters was in a sense playing into his hands and if the bodies were left undisturbed they might yet be found by a British patrol; but the bullion in his own pack would be the give-away when a search was made, which it was certain to be. In the event the discovery was made within the next couple of minutes, when one of the wagoners came upon a bar fallen from one of the men's sacks. After that the whole area was searched and the bullion was carried into the back of the wagon. Pieters' eyes were gleaming with satisfaction.

'A sad loss for Buller,' he said.

'And a gain to a renegade –'

'No renegade in your sense, Halfhyde. I am sorry for the earlier deception, but I'm not British. I'm Dutch, and from the Netherlands.'

'I see. What do you propose to do with the bullion, may I ask? In its present form it's scarcely negotiable, is it?'

'Not in South Africa,' Pieters said, 'but it's not intended to remain here.' He shaded his eyes, looking towards the east, into the sun that by now was spreading its heat across the parched land. 'Aboard the wagon, if you please, Halfhyde. We shall lose no time now.' As Flannery held a revolver against Halfhyde's backbone and pushed him towards the tail-board, he added, 'You'll find a surprise in the wagon, one that may decide you to give us no trouble – in case harm should come.'

v

To find the girl had been an immense shock. The pressure of Flannery's revolver inhibited his furious reaction. He stared down at her, all kinds of emotions passing through his mind, all kinds of doubts and anxieties. There were so many questions to be asked and answered. He stumbled as the horses started up and the wagon gave a lurch. His bound wrists allowed him no chance to recover his balance and he fell in a heap beside Victoria. He saw tears on her cheeks and a brightness in her eyes. Mahon roughly untied the gag.

92

She tried to smile. Her voice broke as she said, 'Hullo, mate. Sorry.'

'Sorry for what?'

'For being a sucker, I reckon. Getting myself into this. You too.'

He said, 'You've got me into nothing, Victoria. I've been following my orders – until now at all events. How did you get involved – what's happened to the *Glen Halladale*, and Edwards?'

'On the way to Durban so far as I know,' she said. 'Maybe arrived by now. Me, I got kind of shanghaied ashore in Cape Town.'

She told him the whole story; neither Mahon nor Flannery made any attempt to stop her. They were both confident by the look of them, sure enough that there was nothing Halfhyde could do either now or in the future. Halfhyde listened in growing incredulity as Victoria told him where Flannery and Mahon had come from: the then convict decks of the *Glen Halladale* from Plymouth, men who had known about the bullion before arrival at the Cape. She knew nothing of what was to happen to the bullion now; and Halfhyde's questions to the men remained, not surprisingly, unanswered. However, after the wagon had lumbered for some half-hour into the sun, heading east – for the coast, Halfhyde wondered? – Pieters, sitting alongside the driver, called through into the back.

'Come up in front, if you please, Halfhyde. Flannery, give the officer a hand.'

With some difficulty Halfhyde was assisted up and onto the box to sit between Pieters and the driver. He was desperately thirsty and hunger was starting to bother him as well. As if anticipating his needs, Pieters reached down for a water-bottle and held it out, then remembered the bound wrists. He unscrewed the stopper and held the bottle to Halfhyde's lips, giving him a mouthful only.

'We must use it with care, Halfhyde, as you'll understand. This is an inhospitable country for the most part . . . . For me, both the Boer farmers and the British are welcome enough to it in equal shares.'

'I didn't fancy you were a patriot,' Halfhyde said drily.

'Well, as a Dutchman I'm to some extent aloof.'

'The Boers are your people, as the British settlers are ours, are they not?'

Pieters laughed and shrugged. 'We'll not go into that. I act largely for myself, though this time it's not just myself that's concerned, but other interests also.' He seemed to change his tack suddenly. 'Tell me about yourself, Halfhyde. Tell me what happened – when you met the Boers. And tell me – this much intrigues me – why they left you with the gold. I would have thought that an unlikely proposition to say the least. Tell me also what little Mr Bewdley is doing, risking his neck in the field.'

'You must ask Mr Bewdley that.'

'Very well, I shall do so shortly.'

Pieters looked behind him down into the covered back of the wagon. Bewdley was sitting slumped against the side, in a corner, with his scuffed and dusty bowler hat on his knees. He hadn't uttered a syllable after being pushed at gun-point, like Halfhyde, into the back; he had sat in misery, his head in his hands, his face haggard whenever he looked up: death had not played a large part in his life until now and but for the grace of God he would himself have been one of the poor, riddled bodies lying out in the heat and harshness of the veldt, waiting for the sickly attentions of the birds of prey that would tear and gnaw the flesh from the bones . . . the only violence that had hitherto come into Mr Bewdley's life had been the crushing of his father's body at Fenchurch Street station and that only by proxy, as it were. Not guns, bullets and cold steel but files, dockets and desks had filled his life, and now he felt that that life lay in ruins, shattered by what had happened out on the South African veldt and left him in the hands and at the mercy of wicked men who demonstrably would stop at nothing. Men who had murdered once would murder again and it was perfectly obvious that none of them – he, Lieutenant Halfhyde and Lieutenant Halfhyde's young lady, as she seemed to be by some extraordinary quirk of fate – would be allowed to live to tell the terrible story.

Pieters pressed. 'The Boers, Halfhyde. I'm interested.'

'Why?'

'I have my reasons.'

'And I have mine for not telling you.'

Pieters raised an eyebrow. 'Your orders?'

'Yes, they preclude me.'

'There are harsher things than orders. You won't want trouble to come to yourself. Or to the girl.'

Stiffly Halfhyde said, 'I shall never go against my orders, nor my country.'

'Well, that remains to be seen. Also, I have a feeling that even if you should prove a man of iron, Mr Bewdley may well prove less so.'

'Bewdley is a man of principle –'

'But not, I suggest, of stomach. At this moment, he's a jelly. But I prefer matters to be settled more amicably than by the gun, Halfhyde, or the knife. We are both civilized men, and you know as well as I do that the truth's going to come out in the end. So settle for the easy way, and tell me about the Boers.'

For some moments there was silence apart from the creaking of the wagon's wheels and chassis. Halfhyde stared ahead, mouth shut like a clamp as if symbolically. Then the Dutchman said, 'No? Then perhaps I'll start the ball rolling myself. I judge you to have been taken to Louis Botha's camp. I further judge a certain Commandant Steen to have come to your assistance in escaping.' Halfhyde gave an involuntary jerk of surprise and Pieters said pleasantly, 'I seem to have scored a bull's-eye! Let us now proceed from there, Halfhyde. It's possible you met two of my own compatriots somewhere along the way: Koornhof, and van Buren. Yes?'

Halfhyde blew out a long breath. 'What's your involvement, Pieters?'

Pieters laughed again, gently and with amusement. 'In bribery? Oh yes, I know all about that, too. A plot that miscarried, and miscarried into my hands. Your military

95

leaders are not as clever as they fancied themselves to be, and although they put about many false rumours in regard to the gold and where it was being taken, and for what purpose, they failed to conceal the truth from certain persons –'

'You?'

'Yes, and others.'

'Spies?'

'An unpleasant word, Halfhyde, but –'

'Unpleasant people! All right, so you're in possession of what you regard as certain facts. I don't confirm them – I'm a naval officer of the reserve and act only upon narrow orders the purpose and end result of which are seldom elaborated upon. But since you believe you know so much, why ask me about the Boers' actions in the matter of the gold?'

Pieters said, 'Frankly, I'm more interested in Koornhof and van Buren than in the Boers – now that I have the gold safely in my possession. Koornhof is to act for Commandant Steen, but possibly you know that –'

'Koornhof's dead,' Halfhyde said flatly.

Pieters seemed startled, but only momentarily. 'Dead? How?'

'Shot by the Boer commando that attacked us. The body was taken on to Botha's camp.'

'What did Koornhof tell you?'

'Very little. He hadn't much time.' Halfhyde had no intention of saying anything about the despatch from Major Douglas Haig.

'But he came from the British lines?'

'I imagine he did,' Halfhyde said indifferently, 'since he made his appearance from the direction of Chieveley.'

'And van Buren?'

'I know nothing of van Buren.'

Pieters didn't seem surprised and didn't press on the point. He said, 'I'm prepared to accept that. Van Buren was to have been at Chieveley . . . .' His voice tailed away and then he said abruptly, 'Well, never mind that, it's no concern of yours. But now Buller will begin to worry – when the gold fails to reach the

Tugela, he will be anxious, and may send out a patrol.'

'If you're caught,' Halfhyde said, 'whose side are you going to be on?'

He didn't expect an answer and he didn't get one; soon after this he was put back into the body of the wagon. The heat was appalling and the motion desperately uncomfortable. Flannery sat watchful with his revolver while Mahon slept; after a couple of hours there was a halt to rest the horses and stretch legs. Halfhyde walked up and down with Victoria, still watched closely. Thoughts of escape passed through his mind: but the utter impossibility drove them quickly away. The endless veldt, the tied wrists, the immediate opening of the rifles and revolvers . . . if only a British patrol or a column on the move for the Tugela would appear; but it did not.

The girl remarked on this. 'You'd bloody think someone'd be marching somewhere, wouldn't you, eh?'

'They probably are, Victoria.'

'Why not here, then?' She sounded indignant.

'It's too much to hope for, too easy. The spaces and distances out here – they're enormous, like the Australian bush. Whole armies can move, and have moved, in isolation. And if Buller wants reinforcements they'd most likely come from Durban, not up from the south. They'd march along the Tugela, I imagine – though I'm no foot-soldier, nor military strategist.'

'Durban,' she said, whispering and casting glances towards Pieters, stretched out on the ground in the shadow cast by the wagon. 'Durban . . .'

'What is it, Victoria?'

'Durban's east from here, isn't it?'

'Yes –'

'We're going east. I heard them talking earlier . . . and anyway, I can tell that by the bloody sun.'

He grinned. 'Well done! I'll make you a seaman yet. Or a seawoman.'

'The sea,' she said softly, and gave his arm a squeeze. 'I reckon I've moaned about it, but it's bloody better than this, eh?'

He frowned. He said, 'You're getting at something, but what? Tell me while you have the chance.'

'It's only a thought, mate. But if we're heading east, well, we might meet some British soldiers on the march along the –'

'Not the Tugela. That's where they'll be, or I think they will, but Pieters won't be moving close to the Tugela, you can bet on it.'

'But what if he's heading for Durban?'

'Do you think he is? Have you heard something *en route*, Victoria?'

'Not exactly,' she said. 'That's to say, nothing too bloody definite. But I got the idea that bloke wants to get out of bloody South Africa, get the gold out anyway. He can do that, from Durban, can't he?'

'I suppose so. If he has a handy ship waiting. No master who wasn't in his pocket would take his dirty gold aboard, that's for certain.'

She said, 'The *Glen Halladale*'s there, or will be soon, and I reckon Pieters knows it.'

vi

When the rest period was over, Mahon took the reins and the previous driver joined the others in the back of the wagon, where he settled down to sleep. The motion began again, the sickening lurch over the open veldt. Halfhyde, with Victoria snuggled down by his side, had been given much to think about. The gold, back again to the *Glen Halladale*, to bring more trouble? The idea was a plausible enough one; Halfhyde, if not in Pieters' pocket, was certainly in his control currently. The fact of his being so could be said to give Pieters the availability of a ship, with himself sailing as master under duress, a case of history repeating itself. Halfhyde's mind went back to the voyage previous to his run out to the Cape, the voyage he'd made from Sydney to Queenstown in County Cork, the voyage that had first brought Victoria Penn into his life and his emotions, and had brought also the monstrous gun-runner Porteous Higgins and his tongueless henchman, Gaboon, men

98

of cunning who had not found it too difficult to control a shipmaster aboard his own ship and force his compliance with their orders. Higgins had proved it could be done, though in the end he hadn't profited by his proof. Could Pieters have similar ideas? If so, where would he try to take the gold? There had been no clarity in his statements so far, and Halfhyde had no real idea either of his motives or his loyalties. There had been something that had suggested Pieters wasn't working entirely for his own ends, selfish ends, but for a larger party. But who? Commandant Steen and the Boers, or van Buren whose allegiances were also in doubt?

No doubt time would tell; and meanwhile the wagon was continuing easterly. Durban could very well be the end of the track, and it certainly would not be impossible to get the gold through into the docks if a determined man set his heart on the job. For one thing, the authorities wouldn't be looking for a dust-shrouded covered wagon. No one knew about that. The naval guns' crews were dead to a man. Plenty of traffic would be moving in and out of the docks: supplies of food, arms and ammunition, cavalry horses, infantry and field-guns and wagons by the hundred.

Victoria was asleep now.

Halfhyde looked down at her; her face, though pale as death, was happier. It could be simply that sleep had brought a balmy peace and was knitting up the ravelled sleeve of her care. Or it might not be that. It could be his presence; glumly, he feared that it was. She had implicit faith in him, was wholly reliant upon him. She was, it seemed, to be his eternal incubus.

NINE

Now they were through the Drakensberg with its many passes and into Natal; they had skirted Estcourt, crossing the railway line that ran from Durban to Ladysmith, after which they had turned south-eastwards. It seemed fairly certain that Pieters was heading for Durban, though he had said nothing of his destination to Halfhyde. There was now evidence of British troops, and the three prisoners were gagged and watched more closely than ever. Greetings were exchanged with marching soldiers and once the wagon was halted by a British officer and after some perfunctory questions allowed to proceed on its way without any investigation of what might be in the covered back. Halfhyde, for Victoria's sake forbearing to lash out with his feet and create a noisy disturbance, found no reason to applaud British military efficiency, but recognized that for his part he had already put his own duty second to Victoria's well-being. In any fighting she would have been the first to suffer, and Halfhyde was determined to find a way that would not put her at risk.

The next day, towards nightfall, the wagon rumbled into a small township and stopped finally in a yard behind a tall warehouse. A man came out from the warehouse and approached the wagon. Pieters got down from the box and went away with this man while the others remained in their places. There was a curious smell in the air. Ten minutes later Pieters came back and told everyone to get down. When he emerged covered by Flannery's revolver, Halfhyde saw that the yard was a square formed by four warehouses and that a number of other wagons, open ones mostly, their shafts empty, stood waiting, presumably for their loads. With Victoria and Mr Bewdley he was pushed towards one of the buildings, through a doorway into a long, high storeroom filled to capacity with bales of animal hides that stank to heaven.

The three were marched the length of the store and were halted at the end, where another armed man was waiting by an open trapdoor.

'Right,' Flannery said. 'Down you go.'

Halfhyde went first, feeling with his feet for the rungs of a vertical ladder leading down into darkness. Victoria went next, then Bewdley, and then the trapdoor was dropped into place and heavy bolts were run across.

ii

'I wonder where we are, Lieutenant Halfhyde.'

'I've no idea.'

'Do you think we're in Boer hands again?'

'I don't even know that, Mr Bewdley. Your guess is as good as mine. The township must be British, I imagine, but every town can hold Boer sympathizers.'

'Yes, indeed, that's so. Pieters himself is clearly on the side of the Boers, so –'

'We can't be certain even of that – not yet. There are many mysteries.'

'But surely', Mr Bewdley said, 'if he were on the *British* side, then he would have taken the gold direct to General Buller or the man van Buren – wouldn't he?'

Halfhyde gave a sigh. 'Once again, I don't know. Nothing's straightforward. Gold is gold, Mr Bewdley. Its value distorts both men and their actions.'

'I don't really follow that. Not in regard to Pieters' loyalties –'

'Then never mind, Mr Bewdley. At this stage it's pointless to speculate. We've simply to await what happens next, and then act accordingly – that's if we can act at all. As to that, I shall find a way, but not until the time is right.'

'I'm sure you will, Lieutenant Halfhyde, I'm sure you will. The navy's always able to cope, to improvise, and is our sure shield.'

'Thank you, Mr Bewdley.'

In the darkness Halfhyde, sitting with his back to a wall in the confined space, gave an ironic bow towards the direction of the little man's voice. At the moment he could see no light either physical or mental; and he was extremely weary from the jolting progress of the wagon. The girl was sound asleep, bringing a degree of cramp to his left arm and shoulder, her hair brushing lightly across his face. It was fortunate she was so tired, he knew; on her first entry to the enclosed space she had been tearful, hysterical, feeling the effects of claustrophobia, and he had had difficulty in calming her, but in the end she had drifted off and the tears had dried on her face. Halfhyde himself could find no sleep; his thoughts gave him no rest, and he realized that Bewdley was in a similar state. From time to time Bewdley spoke to himself, immediately apologizing for a weakness. Perhaps to prevent further lapses, he began after a while to impart more about his early life before the terrible accident to his father. He and his father had been close, had gone shrimping together at Southend-on-Sea, bicycling there on occasional Saturday afternoons or Sundays after chapel; the family had been Methodists in spite of his father's liking for porter and the odd drop of gin. The young Bewdley used to sing in chapel and had very much enjoyed doing so. After his father had met his death there had been no more shrimping; his mother had had to be kept and there wasn't a spare ha'penny. Even the bicycles had had to go, producing the large sum of ten bob the pair to pay four weeks' rent on the two rooms they'd found when the railway company repossessed their railway cottage. What they wouldn't have been able to do with all that gold . . . . Inevitably Mr Bewdley came back to the gold.

'It's so much on my conscience, Lieutenant Halfhyde. I've failed, you see.'

'Nonsense! If you've failed, then so have I, and no blame

attaches to you.'

'That's very generous of you, Lieutenant Halfhyde, very generous indeed and is appreciated, but I shall continue to hold myself responsible. So many things have been my fault, you see, and one can't forget . . . . Once I was responsible for losing a whole half-holiday's catch of shrimps. I left them in a shelter behind the beach, and when we cycled back they'd vanished. I have never forgotten my father's dreadful disappointment, all that work and the looking foward to supper . . . .'

iii

The trapdoor was opened up, how many hours later Halfhyde had no idea. Flannery and Mahon were there with their revolvers, and another man was carrying a lantern which he held over the trapdoor.

Flannery said, 'Out.'

Stiffly, Halfhyde got to his feet, giving a hand to Victoria. They climbed the ladder towards the revolvers' muzzles. Once again they were marched along the warehouse, between the stacked hides, and out into the yard. It was dark but there was a hint of coming dawn in the east towards the coast, which Halfhyde believed was not far off. They were taken across the yard to one of a number of open vehicles like brewers' drays with bullock teams standing patiently between the shafts, vehicles that were being loaded with bales of hides from the warehouses. Looking around, Halfhyde could see no sign of the covered wagon in which they had travelled through the Drakensberg.

Pieters was standing talking to a bearded man wearing a short-crowned black hat, coatless but with a waistcoat over his shirt. This man was flourishing a sheaf of documents which, as Halfhyde watched, he handed to Pieters.

Halfhyde and the others were taken to join the Dutchman, who gestured them towards one of the loading carts, then walked over for words with Halfhyde as he stood waiting by the side of the vehicle, guarded by Flannery and Mahon.

Pieters said, 'As you see, a consignment of animal hides, as per cargo manifest for loading aboard a ship in the docks at Durban –'

'What ship?'

'That you will find out in due course. For now, it doesn't concern you. What does concern you is that you and the girl and Mr Bewdley will go aboard with the hides – nicely concealed until you're safely in the ship's hold –'

'And the bullion?'

'That also does not concern you. For now all you need to worry about is obeying my orders to the letter. Those orders are that you shall keep completely silent as we approach the docks. You will give no words of warning to the soldiers guarding the gates. If you do, then you'll die instantly – and the girl, too, will suffer. She travels with me. You and Bewdley will go with Flannery and Mahon, and I say again, you will go in silence.'

Pieters lifted a hand at Flannery, who closed in with Mahon. Halfhyde and Bewdley were told to get aboard the dray, already half loaded. In the centre a space just big enough to take the four men had been left between the bales of hides. As they got down into it the temporarily suspended loading was resumed, with planks being laid across the top of the central space and more and more bales being hoisted in to complete the full load. Before his view of the yard was cut off, Halfhyde had seen Pieters escorting Victoria to another hide-loaded dray.

A few minutes later the teams were whipped up and the vehicles rumbled away towards Durban.

iv

It was a long way, longer than Halfhyde had expected. Pieters had his confederates well outside the port. It was an appalling journey along rutted tracks, the dray swaying from side to side, climbing at times and sometimes giving the feeling that it must topple over as it took bends, however slowly. The stench of the animal skins was formidable, and the air was as close as it had been in the small space beneath the trapdoor. Halfhyde felt physically sick, almost to retching point, and Mr Bewdley was taking deep breaths as though to calm rising panic. No one spoke; at this stage there seemed little point in saying anything other than to offer up prayers for their speedy release from suffering. But eventually, the movement slowed and ceased, the dray jolting to a stop, and Halfhyde heard voices, clearly through the gaps in the stowage of the cargo. Pieters' voice, calling down from the box of the leading vehicle, evidently to the gate guard.

'Animal skins as per cargo manifest, for the barque *Parramatta* for Bombay, under sailing orders for this evening's tide.'

'Your papers?'

There was a pause and then Halfhyde heard the tread of heavy boots passing along the side of the dray. Something, probably a bayonet, was being pushed at intervals in between the bales, but nothing came near the four men. The boots moved away again and there was another pause, then some more talk that Halfhyde couldn't catch, followed by a shout.

'Righto, in you go, mate.'

A British voice, a soldier's voice – so near and yet so far. Halfhyde gritted his teeth. Somewhere aboard this road convoy would be the bullion; he had only to call out for the gate guard to halt the vehicles and it would be all up with Pieters. He and Bewdley would die and so would Victoria: Pieters, he believed, would make a bloody fight of it, right to the end, and would take his revenge. But duty was duty and no one's life could be allowed to stand in the way of it. The prodding bayonets had shifted some of the nearby bales, just a little, just enough for chinks of daylight to filter through, and Halfhyde could see the face next to his: Mahon, the one with the scar. Mahon was watching him. Halfhyde opened his mouth to shout but Mahon was too fast. Hands went round his throat and squeezed hard, and at the same moment Flannery lifted his revolver and brought the muzzle down hard and viciously on Halfhyde's temple.

The laden vehicles moved on unimpeded into the docks.

v

When Halfhyde came round he was lying on a mattress in

surroundings that though hazy and tending to swing in circles around his head were in some way familiar. After a moment he realized that someone was bathing his head with cold water and bending over him and that it was Victoria.

In a weak voice he said, 'You.'

'Me all right, mate. Just take it easy. And thank God you're through.'

'Where am I?'

'Aboard a ship,' she said.

'What ship?'

'The bloody *Parramatta*, going to Bombay. The ship is, I mean. Not us, not Pieters. Not the gold.'

'I don't understand.'

'I don't suppose you do, mate. I don't reckon I do, not really. Don't worry yourself about it for now. Get fit first.'

'I'm all right,' he said.

'You're not, mate. You've had a nasty blow.'

He said, 'Just tell me, Victoria. Tell me what you do know. I've got to have the facts.'

'All right,' she said, and gave a sigh of weariness and worry. 'Pieters – he had this mate who ran the animal skin outfit – he happened to have a dinkum cargo for the *Parramatta* and Pieters took advantage of it. So you and your Mr Bewdley, you were hoisted aboard the *Parramatta* in the cargo slings. So was the gold.'

'But didn't you say –'

'Right, I meant it's not *staying*, nor us either. It was just a blind, being put aboard here. It and us, we're due to move out after the *Parramatta* sails on the tide, which seems to be after dark tonight.'

'Where do we move to, Victoria?'

'You'll never bloody guess, mate.' She took a deep breath, and went on, 'The *Glen Halladale*. She leaves on the same tide. Genuine . . . Pieters' cobber, the animal-skin bloke, he knows the sailings – has a mate in the dock authority. Mr Edwards, he's under orders to leave for Liverpool in ballast and pick up army stores for the Cape. Out and back again. Only I don't reckon he'll be making *that* trip, somehow.'

'Why?'

She said, 'Just because. I don't know anything more, but I don't reckon Pieters'll be taking the gold to England. Do you? Just think about it.'

His brain was fuzzy; he wasn't co-ordinating as he should. He asked about Bewdley; Bewdley, she said, was all right up to a point: he was in a bad way mentally.

'In a bloody awful tizzy,' she said, 'wringing his hands and bloody nearly crying. Doesn't like the idea of being shanghaied. No more do I. What do we do about it, eh, mate?'

Halfhyde said, 'I've no ready answer, Victoria. We'll take it as it comes, that's all.'

She was looking at him reflectively and with understanding. She said, 'Look, mate. You're due to go back aboard the *Glen Halladale*. God knows what's in the wind, but that part we do know about. And you – you're not sorry. Are you?'

He managed a grin. 'No.'

'So you'll let that happen, right?'

'Probably. Unless something else happens first.' He knew one thing for sure, one thing that was paramount to him: he was a seaman and he was at his best aboard a ship. Once back, things might move in his direction – at any rate he would have a better chance. This, Victoria seemed to understand. She would be glad enough herself basically: the *Glen Halladale* had become home.

Later in the day another man came aboard and after a conference with Pieters was taken to see Halfhyde. The man's name was van Buren.

TEN

'So you are Halfhyde.' There was a strong Dutch accent. 'I have heard of you from past days, my friend, the days of the gun-running into Ireland by the man Higgins.' Halfhyde offered no comment and van Buren went on, 'Now you will be wondering what the future holds for you.'

'I understand Pieters intends to board my own ship, the *Glen Halladale*.'

'Yes, that is correct. That is all you know?'

Halfhyde nodded. He said, 'It was you who was supposed to take delivery of the bullion at Chieveley, was it not? I'd much like to know what game you're playing, Mr van Buren.'

Van Buren smiled. He was a good-looking man, well-dressed, urbane, with the air of a diplomat. 'I'm afraid I'm not playing for Britain, Halfhyde, but I dare say you've already seen for yourself that Pieters is not on your side. The bullion was never intended to remain within the control of Sir Redvers Buller on the Tugela. I believe you met Commandant Steen, the –'

'The traitor. Yes, I met him –'

'And you're aware that it was Steen's intention that the gold should be taken to the Netherlands, to await his arrival there. Well, that is where it is being taken, to the Zuider Zee for the port of Amsterdam, aboard your ship. I regret that you'll sail under duress, Captain Halfhyde.'

'Duress or not, it'll never reach the Zuider Zee. It'll be intercepted . . . true, there's a lot of water between Durban and the Netherlands, and a ship's a small thing to find, but the Channel's narrow enough and by the time we reach it two and two will have been put together and we'll be awaited by a squadron of the British fleet. Surely you've thought of that?'

Van Buren was still smiling. 'But of course! My dear Halfhyde, the bullion won't be missed at all. That has been very adequately arranged. Always Sir Redvers Buller has wished to keep his distance from the gold, from the whole concept of the bribery, which was never his idea but that of clever persons, staff officers from certain commands. Buller was against it from the start –'

'I'm not surprised! So the fact that it's gone won't be disturbing him?'

'I don't believe you understand, Halfhyde. Buller doesn't know it has gone, and neither does anyone else in the British camp. The handling of the gold was to be left to me – me alone. The arrangements have always been in my hands. And now I am doing what I was supposed to do, taking the consignment to Amsterdam. So, you see, there will be no trouble.'

'But you're not taking it to Amsterdam for the benefit of Commandant Steen.'

'Why do you think that?'

Halfhyde shrugged. 'It seems obvious enough when one considers Pieters and his friends out of Dartmoor, convicts whom I brought out to South Africa under military orders, for the formation of labour battalions. It seems obvious that you and they are acting together – to defraud a traitor of what he's been promised.'

ii

The day passed towards evening. There was no sign of Pieters or his friends and no further contact with van Buren, who had left the cabin soon after Halfhyde's last statement, neither confirming nor denying what Halfhyde regarded as the obvious.

Yet, on reflection as the hours passed, it was perhaps not quite so obvious as it had at first seemed. Certainly collusion had been implicit in the fact that whilst *en route* in the covered wagon after being apprehended by Pieters, Halfhyde had gathered that van Buren was expected to provide some help in the diverting of the gold from its proper purpose, or for its onward passage to wherever it was going; but even so, something nagged. Van Buren had struck Halfhyde as a cold enough fish and entirely self-centred, a man without any principle or loyalty. The same could, of course, be said of Pieters, who hadn't shrunk from the wholesale killing of the naval ratings back on the veldt. If there was collusion it might not endure. Very likely each intended to double-cross the other, in which case the weeks ahead on the long passage to the Zuider Zee could well prove interesting. Also dangerous: neither van Buren nor Pieters would feel able to risk subsequent talk on the part of those who would know too much. So the hatchet would stand perpetually poised over his own head and Victoria's and could one day descend.

Halfhyde was unable to keep his fears from the girl: she had already worked it out for herself. But she came up with another angle.

'Maybe it's not so straightforward,' she said.

'It's scarcely that in any case.'

'You know what I mean, mate. Not just the bloody value, see?'

'What, then?'

'Well, the idea behind it all. The bribery. This Steen, he's still been bribed even if he's lost the loot, right?'

'Right.'

'I was thinking along those lines, that's all. Maybe van Buren *does* mean to make a handover.'

'To Steen?'

'I wasn't thinking of Steen. Maybe to someone else . . . like the Dutch government. So as to drop Steen in it, and –'

'And show up the British, d'you mean?'

She nodded. 'Yes, I reckon that might be it. The British can't win by fighting so they come up with something dirty. It wouldn't look very good, would it, eh? You said it was all supposed to be dead secret –'

'Yes, of course. But only as between us and Steen – by us I mean the military command and the Cape secretariat, for immediate military reasons with regard to Ladysmith. I don't suppose it would have mattered if it had come out afterwards.'

'I don't know so much. Dirt's dirt. We'd look a load of double-dealers to all the colonies that've sent troops. Anyway,' she added after a pause, 'Ladysmith's still under siege, isn't it, and it's got to be kept secret till all that's over.'

He gave her a sudden look. 'And van Buren's Dutch. So's Pieters. Both acting against the British interest. You're saying they might mean to blow the whole thing, get Steen arrested by Botha, and leave Buller without his expected help from inside?'

'I reckon they might. *And* do no good to poor old Buller's fighting reputation.'

Halfhyde paced the cabin, listening to the armed guard doing the same thing outside the locked door. A word with Bewdley might help him to sort out his mind, but Bewdley had not been seen since Halfhyde had recovered from the blow to his head. According to Victoria, he had been taken to a separate cabin, also under guard. In any case, whatever the extent of his mental turmoil, Halfhyde knew there was currently nothing he could do. If van Buren meant to show up the British he couldn't be prevented; but he was not likely to do that before his stolen booty had disappeared into Holland, from where he would, presumably, take it to the anonymity of eastern Europe. He wouldn't sacrifice his security too soon and the siege of Ladysmith might go on for many months yet. The war had bogged down, was static in its various sieges, the great British Army still floundering before the simple Boer farmers.

iii

Now it was dark, and the tide was full, and the *Parramatta* was ready to get under way, her masts crossed with their yards and the canvas ready to be shaken out when they came clear of the port and picked up a wind to take them north for the Mozambique Channel and the run across the Indian Ocean for

Bombay. The sounds of preparation had come to Halfhyde in the confines of the cabin: the tramping of feet, the banging of heavy blocks on the poop and along the waist, the shouts of the mates and the bosun, the snatches of shanties. Then the hoot of the steam tug was heard approaching, and there was a hail from aft in acknowledgment. Fifteen minutes later the barque was coming off the quay under tow and heading for the harbour entrance to make out into the Indian Ocean beneath a bright moon and a great cluster of stars that hung like lanterns in a violet sky. Glad to be back at sea under any conditions, Halfhyde looked from the cabin port as the lights of the town grew smaller and more distant. As the harbour and the anchorage were left behind, Pieters came down for him. After the pilot had disembarked and the steam tug had cast off to chug noisily back into Durban, Halfhyde and Victoria were taken to the waist where a boat had been swung out on the davits and was ready for lowering. Bewdley was waiting by it, under guard, looking lost and lonely, twisting his bowler hat in his hands. Pieters went aft to the poop for a word with the *Parramatta*'s master, returning with van Buren. Flannery and Mahon and the two men who had done most of the driving of the covered wagon came up from the saloon to join the others.

Not far astern and a little to starboard of the *Parramatta*, Halfhyde saw his own ship, also dropping her pilot and dispensing with her tug. As he looked towards the *Glen Halladale* the *Parramatta*'s master took up a megaphone and shouted across the water.

'*Glen Halladale* ahoy!'

It was Edwards' voice that responded. The master of the *Parramatta* called across that he had Captain Halfhyde aboard for transfer to his own ship together with a small amount of cargo for Liverpool; and he proposed sending away a boat to go alongside the *Glen Halladale*. Edwards was requested to have a party standing by his derrick for a fast transfer.

Edwards' shout came back across the dark water: 'Aye, aye!' Halfhyde could well imagine his first mate's astonishment: Edwards would be wondering why the embarkation couldn't have been made while the ships were still alongside the quay in Durban; to Halfhyde himself the explanation was simple enough: no fracas could have been permitted inside the port, with a pilot expected to board and a steam tug standing by. Out at sea it would be an easy seizure, the presence of Halfhyde himself lending authority to the proceedings. By the time Edwards and the deckhands had realized what was happening it would be too late. Victoria was the guarantee that Halfhyde wouldn't give trouble: Pieters himself was alongside her and Halfhyde had caught the glint of steel pressed against her side.

Pieters gestured to Mahon. He and Flannery began man-handling a number of heavy leather bags into the boat as it swung from the davits; Halfhyde guessed that these contained the bullion. The two ships lay heaving on the water with their yards laid aback. The *Glen Halladale* had drifted closer, and the moon was bright, and Halfhyde could see clearly along her deck. Edwards stood on the poop, legs braced as the ship rolled a little to the swell, hands behind his back. As soon as the bullion had been off-loaded Halfhyde, Bewdley and Victoria were ordered into the boat, Pieters and the other men keeping as close as possible, the boat was lowered into the water, the blocks of the davits were cast off and the boat's crew pulled across the water towards the *Glen Halladale*. As they came alongside below the windjammer's lee bulwarks, lines were sent down and the boat was secured fore and aft and the derrick was swung out.

Halfhyde was ordered to disembark first, with Flannery and Mahon close behind. They went up the jumping-ladder that the *Glen Halladale*'s bosun had sent down.

Edwards said, 'Welcome back, sir.'

'I'm glad to be so, Mr Edwards. With reservations.'

The first mate was looking puzzled at what appeared to be a larger-than-expected boarding-party; but he asked no questions. Behind Flannery and Mahon, Pieters came up with Victoria, the last two men remaining to tend the gold into the slings of the derrick. When this had been done and the hoist was being swung clear and up, they embarked and the *Parramatta*'s boat was cast off to be pulled away to its own ship.

'Now, Mr Edwards,' Pieters said. 'There are changed orders for you. I think you should be put in possession of certain facts. I suggest you come below to the saloon, while Captain Halfhyde himself gets the yards trimmed and the ship under way – for the Hook of Holland.'

Edwards was completely bewildered. He looked across at Halfhyde.

Halfhyde said, 'Follow Mr Pieters' suggestion, if you please, Mr Edwards.'

The first mate shrugged and turned away for the ladder down to the saloon alleyway.

iv

No guns had as yet been produced, though that could happen at any moment. Halfhyde, as he passed his orders to the second mate, knew it could not be long before the current peace, apparent peace, was shattered. It seemed to be Pieters' hope that there need be no fuss, that master and mates would comply so as to avoid bloodshed, and indeed that would be Halfhyde's course until such time as he saw his way clear to re-establish his position and assume control in what was in basis a piratical operation. He had no wish to bring death to any of his crew, who were all unarmed apart from a ready availability of belaying-pins and such, for what use they would be against the Dutchmen's armoury. It would, he fancied, be in the interest of everyone if the facts were kept dark until he was ready to act; but he had little hope that that could be long achieved. There were going to be frictions, and the weapons would show – or anyway the mailed fist would. In that respect Victoria Penn would most likely prove the catalyst: the girl had a loud voice when she wished to use it, and was apt to put her point of view, or her complaints, with Australian vigour. And Mr Bewdley – it would not be long before the deckhands noted the little man's nervous demeanour and that would start the galley telegraph working on a thousand speculations. Such men as Bewdley were rare sights aboard a windjammer.

With all sail set to the royals and a fair wind blowing, Halfhyde ordered the course south-easterly to take the ship down into the Roaring Forties. Before leaving the *Parramatta* there had been discussion between Halfhyde, Pieters and van Buren as to the route for the Hook of Holland and the Zuider Zee. It would be no use making north into the Mozambique Channel in the wake of the Bombay-bound *Parramatta*, steering thence for Cape Guardafui and the Gulf of Aden for the passage through the Suez Canal into the Mediterranean: vessels under sail could not use the canal except perhaps under tow of a steam tug, and neither van Buren nor Pieters would hear of this in any case, as they couldn't risk the presence aboard of the canal pilot for the long run from Suez to Port Said nor the attentions of the Egyptian port authorities at either end. Nor would they risk sailing back towards the Cape of Good Hope and possible interception if anything had gone wrong. Halfhyde had made the obvious point that the only alternative was a very long one – the long, long haul before the westerlies for the Leeuwin, across the Southern Ocean below Australia and New Zealand for Cape Horn, and then the passage of the South Atlantic for the Channel and the northern seas. But speed, they said, was not vital. Once away from Durban and South African waters they had all the time in the world. The important thing was to avoid all shore contact so far as possible. So the course had been agreed for Australian waters and the west-east passage of the Horn ... and if they should enter a port *en route*, and make contact with a pilot or customs, then, Halfhyde believed, his chance might come. Of course, van Buren would scarcely permit an entry and on the face of it there would be no essential grounds on which to do so: the *Glen Halladale* was fully stored and provisioned for the voyage to Liverpool with reserve stores against a delayed arrival and, unlike the steamers, she had no need to take bunkers. But Halfhyde believed he could back his own ability to fake up some convincing navigational reason.

Meanwhile it was a fine, clear night; the wind, though light, was cool and refreshing, blowing away the dust and heat and flies of the land. Halfhyde paced the poop, keeping an eye on the set of the sails, watching the wake streaming away astern. Much thought, much planning, lay ahead; but it was early days and they had time in hand. Halfhyde was determined that Pieters was not going to get away with his schemes, determined that a murderer would hang in the end. He thought of Petty Officer Dunning and the seamen gunners, dead on the veldt. Would the bodies be found – and if they were found, would the military come to the right conclusions as to how and why they had died? Would a connection with the gold be seen in time for action to be taken – or was the whole affair too secret for its own good, too secret for speedy communication and elucidation?

These were imponderables. There was absolutely no reliance to be placed on his earlier hypothesis to van Buren that the *Glen Halladale* would be intercepted by a British warship. It was going to be up to himself alone.

A few minutes later, the first mate came up the companion ladder from the saloon alleyway and approached Halfhyde.

'Well, Mr Edwards, I take it you've now been told the story?'

'I have, sir. A curious one it is! And dirty.'

'And dangerous. Pieters is a murderer.' He told Edwards of the shooting on the veldt. 'Don't doubt that he'll kill again as soon as he sees a need to, or that the same goes for Flannery and Mahon. I don't know about van Buren but must assume the same. We need kid gloves, Mr Edwards. And low voices.' He gestured aft, towards the wheel. Mahon had come up behind Edwards, and was lounging against the poop rail. 'From now on, we can expect constant company, I think.'

'Yes, sir. Pieters said as much.'

'And the watcher will be armed, of course.'

'Yes. Are you going to pass a warning to the hands, sir?'

'No. Not at this stage.'

'I think you should, sir. The word's going to leak in any case. The steward for one –'

'Yes, I know. But Mathieson's a good man – loyal and reliable. On second thoughts . . . yes, I shall warn Mathieson and tell him to keep his mouth shut amongst the fo'c'sle crowd. And I'll warn the bosun. No one else.'

'But –'

'No one else, Mr Edwards – not beyond Culver, that is.' Culver was the second mate. Halfhyde went on, keeping his voice low, 'If you wish a reason, it's this: gold does many things to many people, as we have reason to know well enough from the outward voyage. I prefer nothing to be known, so far as possible, by men of whose loyalty and morals we can't be entirely sure. I'm aware they were given a clean bill from the naval authorities when they signed articles in Devonport, but that's not good enough for me in this situation. I say again, we need kid gloves, at least for the time being. Keep that well in your mind, Mr Edwards. And remember Miss Penn. I've no wish to put her in danger – and she's the big stick. I think you know me well enough to be sure I shall do my duty when the time comes, but for Miss Penn's sake I shall choose my own moment. There is to be no going off at half cock, and no bulls at gates.'

Edwards didn't like it; his idea would be a full muster of the hands and a concerted attack on Pieters and his men. Halfhyde would have none of that. All told, the opposition amounted to six men, all of them armed. The crew of the *Glen Halladale* totalled twenty-four. It might be possible to rush the poop; hands might be sent aloft to drop down on the poop from the ratlines of the mizzenmast. But Pieters wouldn't be caught napping and the guns would be out, and many good men would die. There had to be a better way.

v

By next forenoon the wind had increased and Edwards, on watch on the poop, had sent down for Halfhyde. Reaching the deck, Halfhyde ordered the royals and topgallants off her and reefs to be taken in the lower sails. The *Glen Halladale*, riding easier thereafter, sped fast over white-capped waves beneath a sparkling blue sky. Flannery was sitting on the deck on the starboard side, near the helmsman, eyes watchful. As Halfhyde paced the poop, Mr Bewdley appeared at the head of the ladder from the saloon alleyway and approached the side, looking green.

Halfhyde called out, 'Lee, Mr Bewdley, lee!'

Bewdley looked round. 'What was that, Lieutenant Half-hyde?'

'The lee side – the *other* side. Seamen never tempt the wind Mr Bewdley, unless they wish their stomachs blown back into their faces.'

Bewdley seemed to take the point, and hurried across to the lee rail. He leaned over and there was a prolonged gush. He hung helpless, shivering. Then he straightened, and walked on shaking legs towards Halfhyde. Keeping his voice low he said, 'We should have words, Lieutenant – or I should say Captain –'

'Yes. We shall walk the deck, Mr Bewdley. The exercise and the fresh air will be the best thing for you. Come with me.' Halfhyde led the way for'ard, down the ladder to the waist. He was aware of Flannery getting to his feet and approaching the fife-rail behind him; already the deckhands would be getting suspicious of the passengers, or would be when the helmsmen passed the word that one or other of them was always present on the poop. Halfhyde walked with long strides; Bewdley's legs twinkled rapidly in the effort to keep pace, one hand clutching at the brim of his bowler hat.

'Have you,' Halfhyde asked, 'anything particular to tell me, Mr Bewdley?'

'No, no. Just a general discussion as to ways and means was what I wanted, Captain. We're entirely in your hands.'

'Or Pieters', currently.'

'Yes. What can we do about it, d'you suppose?'

'For the present, nothing.' Halfhyde repeated what he had said to his first mate. 'These men can achieve nothing until the ship berths in Amsterdam. Except perhaps one thing.'

'What is that, Captain?'

Halfhyde said, 'Tell me this: the gold – van Buren seemed unworried about any pursuit, or any interception in the Channel. Do you agree with him that the disappearance of the gold will not be known to the military or civil authorities?'

Bewdley pondered. 'I think that's likely enough, since for a certainty van Buren will have covered that –'

'Very well. Then how will the situation be affected, in your opinion?'

'The military situation? Buller's plans?'

Halfhyde nodded. 'Yes, Mr Bewdley. Will he delay any attempt at relieving Ladysmith until the gold arrives in his camp? I'd like your assessment, if you please.'

'Well, I don't really know.' Bewdley fingered his chin. 'General Buller has the reputation, undoubtedly, of being a fighting general and often an impetuous one. I have no personal knowledge of him at all, Captain Halfhyde.' He paused. 'Is it an important point?'

'I think it might be. If Buller's strategy is to be dependent on the gold, then the relief of Ladysmith could be delayed and more of the garrison and civilians will die of starvation and disease. Whatever van Buren says, I can't be sure . . . and I must make some assessment, Mr Bewdley.'

'You mean –'

'I mean simply this: if the arrival of the gold upon the Tugela is important, then I should think in terms of dealing with Pieters and his friends as soon as possible, so that I can turn back for Durban. If it is *not* important – important, that is, in Buller's mind, to his strategy as I've said – then I would continue to bide my time in the interest of saving life at sea. In short, Mr Bewdley, it's a choice for me between Ladysmith and my own crew, that's how I see it.'

'Ladysmith's the bigger consideration, Captain Halfhyde.'

'But my seamen are at more positive risk. The gold and the assistance of Commandant Steen are somewhat nebulous. Bullets thudding into my seamen are very real. As for myself, I don't feel much at risk. I'm needed, as master. I'm needed to sail the *Glen Halladale* into the Zuider Zee.'

'And after that, Captain?'

Halfhyde shrugged. 'The situation will not go that far, I assure you. The only question is that of timing.'

'And of course there's Miss Penn . . . .'

Halfhyde looked at him sharply. Mr Bewdley averted his eyes and his face reddened. Halfhyde said, 'Yes, there's Miss Penn.'

'I had a lady friend once,' Mr Bewdley said unexpectedly.

'Really.'

'Yes. A Miss Spender was her name, very genteel, ever so nice. We were going to get married.'

'But you didn't?'

'No. In the end she decided not to.'

'Women are like that, Mr Bewdley.'

'Unpredictable, yes.' Then it all came out in a rush. Miss Spender had jilted Mr Bewdley for another man, one higher up the social scale, a Dutchman who moved in influential circles, both British and Boer. And his name was van Buren.

'*What?*'

'Van Buren, Captain –'

'*Our* van Buren?'

'The very same one, Captain Halfhyde, yes.'

'But – why didn't you say?' Halfhyde stared, wide-eyed, and recalled Bewdley's agitated demeanour the very first time he had mentioned van Buren.

'I saw no reason to, Captain Halfhyde, no reason at all. I had my duty to do and my personal affairs really had no bearing on that. Not until perhaps now. My duty was paramount –'

'Has van Buren recognized you?'

Mr Bewdley shook his head. 'Oh, no. He wouldn't know me from Adam. We never met.'

'But your name –'

'No, no, not that either. Miss Spender was very precise. I was common, you see. I made the mistake of telling her about my old dad, just a railway porter. She was very angry. I realized that she was a snob – her family were in fact little better, I heard since, than mine. She said she never wanted to hear of me again and would never ever even so much as mention my name again. No, she wouldn't ever have told Mr van Buren about me. It would have degraded her, you see, Captain Halfhyde.'

Halfhyde shook his head in bewilderment at such a turn of

events. 'And now?' he asked. 'You spoke of your duty. Now that you are as it were face to face with van Buren, how will your duty be affected?'

'Only that I shall continue to do it, Captain Halfhyde. I just thought I ought now to tell you of my personal involvement, you see, on account of your having your own plans to make.'

Bewdley turned away abruptly and walked back along the deck, staggering a little to the lift of the ship as it lay over to leeward. Flannery was still watching from the poop fife-rail. Halfhyde cursed beneath his breath. There had been some curious quality in Bewdley's voice, some intense undercurrent – passion even, though the words had been prosaic in themselves. Halfhyde believed Bewdley had uttered a warning, but the reference to his, Halfhyde's, own plans made no kind of sense even so.

ELEVEN

Halfhyde moved thoughtfully in Bewdley's wake, back towards the poop. Bewdley's hatred for van Buren clearly ran deep. Miss Spender, or anyway Bewdley's personal humiliation, had never been forgotten. So much was obvious. It was natural enough; but why had the little man brought it out now? Why the implied warning?

Murder? It had sounded almost like that; and Bewdley was an honest man, an ingenuous one who saw things in simple terms: he would perhaps not wish to act wholly behind Halfhyde's back. But reaching the poop ladder, Halfhyde pushed away thoughts of Bewdley and what he might do. He had his other anxieties, the question of the gold and its current holders, and its real value to the fate of Ladysmith. Buller might well be glad that something unpleasant had failed to materialize after all, that the machinations of the Staff had failed. But that would do nothing to lessen Halfhyde's own duty to recover it before it vanished forever in Amsterdam.

In the meantime the situation was a curious one: Halfhyde was in apparent full control, his passengers behaving as such and no more, with the exception of the one continually watching on the poop. Halfhyde was still master aboard his own ship: there was no suggestion otherwise. The one stipulation was his course for the Zuider Zee.

ii

They all took their meals in the saloon, all apparently on good terms, with Halfhyde presiding at the head of the table, waited on by the steward. Van Buren was a good conversationalist; and at the first midday meal he talked much about the war in South Africa. Great Britain, he said when the steward had withdrawn to his pantry, was showing the evil face of imperialism, of an arrogant disregard for all other races and communities.

Halfhyde said, 'I understand you're in good standing with the British authorities.'

'Yes.'

'And a traitor. One of ours to match Commandant Steen.'

Van Buren shrugged. 'If you wish to make the point and the comparison, Captain.'

'I can make no other.' Halfhyde glanced across at Bewdley, who had not joined in the conversation but kept his eyes on his plate, never once looking up at van Buren. Bewdley was pale, and there was a shake in his fingers as he ate, as though the strain of being in the company of Miss Spender's husband was affecting him. Van Buren went on to say that as a Dutchman working for the British his loyalties were in any case split and he could be accused by either side. Basically all he wished to see was an end to the fighting. If it continued it would destroy the country's economy; the land was being ravaged. It was a useless war that the British could never win. Halfhyde reminded van Buren that the Boers had in fact started it, when the Orange Free State had cast in its lot with President Kruger of the Transvaal, and the British colonies were invaded on 10 October of the previous year; but van Buren said that the Boers had been provoked by British procrastination and obduracy and had struck first as a matter of self-defence against what they had known was coming. He said that even if by some miracle the British did force a Boer surrender, world opinion would never permit a dishonourable settlement and the Boers could be nothing but *de facto* winners. The British hold upon South Africa would be loosened. He foresaw self-government for the Transvaal and the Orange Free State, in a much more positive sense than hitherto with no British suzerainty coming into it. Then he made reference to the gold.

He said, 'You know, of course, what it's purpose was to be.'

'I do. And you had got yourself into position to ensure that it never reached General Buller – or Commandant Steen.'

Van Buren nodded. 'That's accurate enough, Captain.'

'And Steen's son, in Buller's hands?'

'An unfortunate casualty of the war.'

'Whom you'll abandon.'

'It has to be so,' van Buren said. There was no flicker of emotion, of regret. In any case, for Steen this would be the price of his betrayal . . . always, Halfhyde thought, there were boots for every foot.

He asked, 'Is anyone else to be abandoned along the way?'

Van Buren returned his look. 'No one, Captain. We are all of us in this together. And for you . . . when we reach Amsterdam and the cargo is safely discharged, you and your ship will be free to sail again. And the gold will be beyond recall by the British authorities.'

The freedom to sail might or might not come about; on balance Halfhyde believed it might, taking into account the last utterance by van Buren: with the bullion safely landed, Halfhyde and the *Glen Halladale* would be redundant in a situation of *fait accompli*. That afternoon Halfhyde took the watch on deck himself, sending the second mate below. Pacing the poop, he pondered the saloon conversation. It was possible that Pieters and the others were merely paid accomplices and the paymaster was the Dutch government itself via van Buren. It was possible they had never been in this for the actual gold, but had been recruited by van Buren on the promise of sanctuary in Holland, a promise that would make a strong appeal to Flannery and Mahon, already-convicted men who would be wanted also by the military authorities for desertion. The death penalty would await wartime deserters, and they could be no worse off whatever happened. Pieters was an adventurer who would turn his hand to any paid activity. But if this hypothesis was wrong and Flannery and the others expected a share of the gold, then it was Halfhyde's guess they were doomed to disappointment and worse: van Buren wouldn't hesitate to kill whenever he had to. But of course the men would be well aware of this; Halfhyde would find no way of driving any wedge between them and van Buren that did not exist already . . . .

In the meantime he was being watched by Mahon: the scarred face looked disinterested as Mahon sat on a bollard beneath the canvas straining from the bolt-ropes, but Halfhyde sensed the taut alertness. The bandits – which was all he could regard them as being – must be expectant of a strike-back at any moment; and all contact between Halfhyde and his officers and seamen had been watched, with one or other of Pieters' men mostly within hearing. The short conversations with Bewdley and Edwards had been the only time, he believed, that nothing had been overheard. The little man, with his pedantic precision and his bowler hat, probably did not appear in the least dangerous.

Nor, it seemed, did Victoria. She would be the hostage when a hostage was necessary; but for the time being she was free to come and go as she pleased. And she came to his cabin that evening, while Pieters was taking his turn as watchman on the poop.

Halfhyde told her of his talk with Bewdley, and the facts about Miss Spender.

'Bloody shame,' she said. 'He's a good little bloke. You really think he might go berserk and kill van Buren?'

'It's a possibility, I think.'

She sniffed. 'Case of good riddance to bad bloody rubbish, eh?'

'Yes. If he ever got the chance to make the attempt I don't suppose I'd stop him! But he won't.'

'Well, I don't know so much,' she said, and went on to underline his own earlier reflection. 'Harmless little bloke like that, he'd get right up close before anyone'd suspect what he was going to do. They're just not worried about him, you've seen that for yourself, mate.' She paused, wrinkling her nose; she was sitting on Halfhyde's bunk and a shaft of evening sunlight came through to glint like gold on the fair hair. 'I reckon you could use him as a whatsit, couldn't you?'

'A whatsit?'

She nodded. 'Like those Greeks . . . .'

'D'you mean a Trojan horse?'

'Yes, that's it, a Trojan horse.'

He laughed. 'The simile's not entirely apt, but I take your point, Victoria. Prime him up to it – to murder?'

'Not murder. We're at war with van Buren's mob. If van Buren gets killed, well, the whole thing falls to pieces, doesn't it?'

'Not necessarily. Don't forget the others. Pieters would take over, and the guns would be in evidence all the way from there. It would only make things more difficult.'

'Van Buren's a start,' she said. 'And we've got to start somewhere, I reckon.'

'But not before we're in all respects ready, Victoria.' Halfhyde was firm on the point, repeating what he had said earlier to his first mate about going off at half cock. He had to be certain of success before he started; and there was a long haul to the Channel and the Hook of Holland.

iii

Once the windjammer had come down into the Roaring Forties, dropping south to pick up the westerlies that blew without cease around the bottom of the world, the weather had changed. It was still bright with plenty of sunshine but it was a good deal cooler and the seas were high, with spindrift blown by the tearing wind into a tablecloth that spread itself to the horizons all around. The *Glen Halladale* made good speed on her track for Cape Leeuwin below the port of Fremantle in Western Australia, the first leg of a voyage that would take them on across the Great Australian Bight, below New Zealand to the passage of Cape Horn and the long run north through the South Atlantic for the Bay of Biscay and the English Channel.

There was a noticeable tension in the ship by this time; the fo'c'sle hands seemed uneasy, knew that all was not well with the afterguard, that the passengers were not quite what they appeared to be. The man constantly on watch on the poop for one thing. Halfhyde, via Edwards, had already passed the word to the steward, Mathieson, and the bosun, giving them the facts but ordering them to keep their own counsel for the time being. He was still uncertain of his crew, could not say for sure which way the cat would jump if any of the weaker elements should get a sniff of gold bullion aboard and see his chance to render a service to van Buren and thereby enrich himself. Seamen were always a mixed bunch; and in Halfhyde's absence Edwards had signed some deckhands in Durban for the run home to Liverpool, replacements for two men who had broken articles in order to enlist in the army and join in the war, and two who had deserted in Durban, probably with hopes of trekking through to the diamond mines and making their fortunes when the war was over. These four new hands were a totally unknown quantity and Halfhyde was as yet not prepared to place any reliance on them.

It was during the second night into the Roaring Forties that Halfhyde came suddenly awake to the alarming sound of a crack like a rifle shot, followed by the furious slatting of canvas. He was out of his bunk and reaching for his oilskin and seaboots when he heard Edwards calling for all hands.

'All hands . . . all hands on deck!'

The call was taken up by Patcham, the bosun, and Halfhyde, as he went fast up the ladder to the poop, heard the clump of feet on deck as the watch below was roused out. Looking aloft as he reached the poop, Halfhyde saw a wild tangle of torn sails and parted rigging dangling dangerously from the foremast.

'Well, Mr Edwards?' he shouted.

Edwards turned. 'A sudden squall, sir, and a funny twist of the wind – the fore t'gallant's gone, along with the t'gallant mast itself by the look of it.'

'All right, Mr Edwards. Get for'ard and take charge. I'll take the poop. Cut away all you can.'

'Aye, aye, sir!'

Edwards went down the ladder to the waist and ran for'ard

past the deckhouses. Already the fo'c'sle hands were swarming aloft, up the ratlines to lie out on the foot-ropes along the upper yards, axes ready to cut away the damaged canvas and woodwork. Halfhyde, looking aloft anxiously, gauging the gale's strength as best he could, believed there was worse to come. The noise was tremendous, the wind singing through the shrouds like a devil's orchestra, twanging at the heavy wires of the stays and backstays and thumping the blocks of the hemp braces. The masts themselves were shaking as though they were strings plucked by some giant hand. Halfhyde took up a megaphone and shouted for'ard.

'Mr Edwards, some hands to take off sail! Send down all t'gallants as fast as you can!'

'Aye, aye, sir.' There was a wave from Edwards.

'And reef all upper tops'ls, Mr Edwards. No time to lose!'

It was to be a terrible task, a case of all hands and the cook, as the saying went. Fingers would be raw, nails would be pulled out by the heavy canvas as it bucketed around from the cringles under the lash of the gale. It was cold now, and the ship was wet with seas that dropped down upon the poop and rushed for'ard along the waist like a flood tide. Men running for the main and mizzen shrouds were swept off their feet to fall into the foaming water and fetch up hard against the bulwarks, and pick themselves up, and start again. Patcham came down from the foremast to take charge at the main, and the second mate, Culver, ran up the ladder from the waist and went to the mizzen shrouds with four seamen behind him. Halfhyde had a word with him before he went aloft; and turned to find Flannery immediately behind him.

Flannery didn't seem worried about the gale and its effects. He said, 'No tricks, Captain.'

Halfhyde stared. 'No tricks? I don't know what you call tricks, but I have my ship to handle. I shall not be inhibited by you or anyone else.'

'If you –'

'If you open your mouth again, Flannery, I shall drop you over the side with my own hands. Now get off the poop.'

'I'll not —'

Halfhyde reached for the man, got a grip of his coat collar and swung him round. He rushed him across the poop towards the hatch and pushed him through with a heavy seaboot against his rump. Flannery gave a yell and crashed down the ladder to the alleyway below. Halfhyde turned his attention back to his ship. The tangle at the head of the foremast looked a little clearer, and as he watched anxiously some of the ripped canvas took off into the night, clearly visible in the moon as it flew out to leeward and vanished into the rearing wave crests; and a moment after this the main topgallant yard crashed down to the deck, broke across the bulwarks, and dropped overboard. Before it went there was a high scream of agony, and in the moonlight Halfhyde saw a man's body bouncing in uncontrollable pain, a reflex action that allowed him no peace. Halfhyde went down to the waist fast, and bent over the man. The face was contorted, there was blood everywhere, and the stomach appeared to have gone, yet the man lived. The tapered end of the topgallant yard seemed to have penetrated the stomach, virtually disembowelling him. Halfhyde picked him up, cradled him in his arms, and fought his way aft through the rushing seas. The door from the waist to the saloon alleyway was swinging wildly on its hinges; Halfhyde caught it on the swing with his shoulder, and butted through to the saloon. He laid the man on the leather settee that ran below the scuttles, and shouted for Victoria.

'Here, mate.'

He turned. She stood in the doorway, looking scared to death. He said, 'Something for you to do, Victoria.'

'What? Is the ship going to be all right?'

'Yes. She'll pull through. This poor devil won't. Do what you can, Victoria.'

'Oh, my God,' she said in a low voice. Her face was almost green. 'Got anything that'll help, have you?'

'No.' His teeth were clenched in a kind of agony of his own. The sole medical assistance aboard any windjammer lay in the box of bandages, ointments, aperients and so on whose use was outlined in a publication known as *The Ship Captain's Medical Guide*. 'There's whisky in my cabin. Let him have as much as he can take.'

He turned away for the ladder; his place was on the poop. As he passed one of the two-berth cabin doors he saw Flannery. The man looked murderous; behind him was Mahon, with a dangerous look on his face. Halfhyde went on his way.

Reaching the poop, he was in time to see the main upper topsail follow the antics of the fore topgallant: the hands hadn't managed to pass the reefs soon enough and the big sail ripped in half as he watched, each half flapping madly along the tearing wind, now at hurricane force, while the piled-up waves crashed and thundered around the man at the wheel. There was a considerable danger of the ship being pooped to such an extent that her stern would be pushed under, and she might well broach-to and come broadside across the seas, unable to steer, to be thrust over until the yardarms met the water and she capsized. For this reason it was vital to maintain steerage way, to keep ahead of the rushing seas astern. In current conditions Halfhyde knew he could not afford to take off too much canvas. He must carry just enough, and pray that the fury of the gale didn't rip it into shreds. He looked aft towards the wheel; there were now two men on it, fighting hard to keep the ship on course before the wind, half drowned each time a sea took the poop, emerging gasping as the water drained away from them. With the ship needing every possible man aloft, Halfhyde was about to take the place of one of the hands at the wheel so that he could be freed to go up the shrouds when, above the storm sounds, he heard what he believed to be a revolver shot from below.

TWELVE

When the first fury of the gale had hit the ship, Mr Bewdley, asleep in his bunk in the cabin that he shared with the second mate, had woken with a start. He was being pressed against the ship's side one moment, flung the other way the next, and the deck beneath him was lifting and falling in a very disturbing manner. Mr Bewdley called out but there was no response from the other bunk: the second mate would no doubt have gone up on deck already. The cabin was in total darkness.

What about the lamp, swinging in its gimbals from the deckhead?

No. He might fumble with the matches, and might cause a fire, one of the sea's most dreaded hazards. Mr Bewdley had read somewhere that it was surprisingly difficult to put out a fire aboard ship and frequently ships had burned to the waterline in no time at all. With a wind such as he could now hear blowing, a fire would be fanned to white heat within seconds.

He must endure the dark. He lay in his bunk, shaking with fright. The noises from the deck had a very dangerous sound, very foreboding indeed, quite terrifying, and the fact of the darkness was making it much, much worse. Mr Bewdley had vivid memories of his voyage out from Liverpool when for the first time he had left England for the Cape. That had been a steamer with engines that thumped remorselessly somewhere beneath his cabin, which had been very hot – unbearably so once the steamer had entered the tropics – and claustrophobic to a remarkable degree. The steamer had produced the miracle of electric light among other wonders, and Mr Bewdley had been able to flood his cabin with harsh brilliance at the snap of a switch in an ornate scutcheon fashioned like half a pineapple. But after one of the coaling ports *en route* his light had refused to work any more, and although he had reported this to the ship's purser no one had ever come along to repair it and Mr Bewdley had had to endure the rest of the long voyage, when he was in his cabin, in darkness not relieved even by a scuttle since he'd had an inboard cabin. One night a drunken man had entered his cabin by mistake and Mr Bewdley, as though seasickness wasn't bad enough, had had a terrible time getting rid of him in the dark.

He had hated the dark then and he hated it now.

In the saloon there might be light and Mr Bewdley, drawn to it like a moth and totally unable to sleep in any case, got out of his bunk with difficulty, fumbled around for his bedroom slippers, found his dressing-gown swaying out from the hook behind the door, and slipped out.

There was indeed light in the saloon – Mr Bewdley could see the loom of it reflecting through the jalousied door onto the white-painted bulkhead outside; but he failed to reach it. The door of van Buren's cabin came open and van Buren stood there, also in his dressing-gown, staring at him.

'What are you up to, Bewdley?'

'Up to? Why, nothing! I – I am merely seeking light.' Van Buren, he saw, had lit his own lamp. Possibly he was as scared as himself. 'I intend going to the saloon.'

'Come in here.' The Dutchman blocked the way for'ard; his words had been an order. 'I want to talk to you. Now's as good a time as any, I fancy.'

'I'm afraid I –'

'I said, come inside.' Van Buren took a grip on Mr Bewdley's arm and pushed him through the doorway. The ship gave a lurch at that moment and Bewdley staggered, lost his balance and fell onto a chair. Van Buren shut the cabin door and stood looking down at him, handsome but threatening – a dangerous man at the best of times in Mr Bewdley's view, he had that sort of face – and the current situation was very far from being the best of times. He stared back at van Buren like a rabbit caught in a beam of light from a poacher's lantern.

'What do you wish to talk to me about?'

'I fancy you know the answer to that.'

Bewdley felt a sudden start: had van Buren after all some intimation of Miss Spender's past? But no; that was far from likely, though surely there could be nothing further to be discussed about the gold now that it was firmly aboard? However, van Buren, feet braced against the abominable slant of the deck, disclosed his interest without waiting for Bewdley to utter.

He said, 'The bullion, Mr Bewdley.'

'Yes?'

'Your position in the secretariat. A responsible one.'

'Certainly.' Mr Bewdley gave a vigorous nod. 'I am – I was – much trusted. I always gave of my very best. I –'

'All right, we'll take the rest as read. My point is this: you will have subordinates who –'

'Yes, indeed. I have – had – a large department.'

'Quite so. Now, as a responsible person, Mr Bewdley, a veritable paragon no doubt of efficiency and capability –'

Bewdley flared up. 'There's no need to laugh at me; I'm in enough of a pickle as it is, seeing what you've done, you and the others.'

'I take your point. Yes, you are certainly in a pickle, and you may be in more of a pickle yet. On the other hand, if you're willing to help me –'

'Most *certainly* not! I know my duty!'

Van Buren laughed. 'Bravely said, if foolishly.' He reached out to the side of his bunk for support as the deck canted even further over. As his arm lifted Bewdley saw that there was something heavy in his dressing-gown pocket and he believed it was a small pistol. He went on, 'When charged with the duty of bullion escort and delivery, you'll have taken into account that something could go wrong. Am I not right?'

'With the bullion?' Bewdley asked cautiously.

'With its safe delivery, yes.'

'Well, of course I did! When gold's on the move –'

'And you'll not have left Cape Town unprepared.'

'Eh?' Mr Bewdley blinked rapidly. 'Come again?'

'Your subordinates, my dear Bewdley. Your chief clerk, perhaps.'

'What about him?'

'He'll have been left – by you – with instructions as to how to proceed in your absence. What to do if, say, you had not made contact by a certain date. Or if someone else had not made contact, someone else concerned with the bullion.'

'That's my business, Mr van Buren.'

'Also mine, now. I want to know what instructions you left behind you. What was to be done if the bullion's journey was, shall we say, interrupted *en route*. You will understand that I need to know – for instance – how far the knowledge of the gold and its purpose has gone.'

'You know that already. You can't have anyone much higher than General Buller I would have thought.'

'I didn't mean that, Mr Bewdley. I meant how far *down*.'

'Down?'

'Yes, down. How far below your own level?'

'Ah.' Mr Bewdley, at whose level, in fact, the knowledge had stopped, paused. He had issued no instructions to his chief clerk or anyone else; he hadn't considered it his place to do so, since he was charged with secrecy. But it was also not for him to give any information to van Buren or the other bandits. However innocuous it might sound, it might help them. Indeed if that hadn't been the case van Buren wouldn't be asking. Mr Bewdley said, 'I really can't say.'

'*Won't* say?'

'No. Oh, no. Can't. I just don't know. Secrecy's secrecy. Anyway, why do you wish to know about the lower levels, eh?'

'Is that not obvious enough, Mr Bewdley? If matters of this kind are known only to the higher echelons they can the more easily be kept quiet – and there are many people in whose interest it will be to keep silent about the gold and its intended purpose. But if too many Toms, Dicks and Harrys also know, then the men at the top may well feel pushed.'

'Pushed, Mr van Buren? I don't follow.'

'Pushed into an attempt to recover it.'

'Which they won't otherwise?' Mr Bewdley remembered Halfhyde prognosticating something along similar lines – that no help could be expected from the authorities . . . but that had been because they wouldn't have known the gold had been as it were kidnapped by van Buren, the man supposed to be doing the negotiating. What van Buren was now suggesting was different . . . . Mr Bewdley's head swam with total confusion made worse by the terrible danger outside. With an effort of will Mr Bewdley tried to concentrate his mind: van Buren believed he would not be so secure, that, after all, the Cape government, or the military staff, might act, once they knew. Possibly even van Buren's own government in the Netherlands might disown him, and if they did that, then Amsterdam might not be the safest place in the world for which to head.

Mr Bewdley became aware after a moment that van Buren was speaking again but he wasn't listening. Unknown to van Buren, Miss Spender was intruding. The never-to-be-forgotten Miss Spender, Dora Spender to be precise and less formal, was back, every detail of her, or such as were known to Mr Bewdley, in his mind. He was seeing dreadful visions of van Buren and Miss Spender, disturbing visions of marital bliss and intimacy: Miss Spender combing her hair while van Buren watched, van Buren kissing Miss Spender, Miss Spender leaning backwards into van Buren's arms, a loving look upon her face. Miss Spender looking cool and elegant at a garden party, escorted by the hand of her handsome, aristocratic husband, no railway porters in his pedigree but a long line of vans. At that thought Mr Bewdley's humorous turn of mind reacted despite himself and he giggled.

Van Buren looked surprised. 'Have I said something funny?'

'Pardon – no. Nothing funny at all, Mr van Buren.'

'Is there something the matter?'

'Matter? Oh no, nothing at all.' Mr Bewdley felt odd but didn't believe he was looking any different from usual, was unaware that his eyes were blazing in the yellow light from the swinging lamp above. Years of frustration were coming to the boil and he felt almost frantic. The early poverty after his old dad had gone, the indignities, the escape from it all to South Africa ruined by Miss Spender's behaviour for which, of course, she could not be blamed but her seducer could. After Miss Spender a life of celibacy, enforced because he had never been able to interest women, celibacy that concealed a nature that was surprisingly hot. A life devoted to work, and even that life now lay in ruins, once again because of van Buren, standing over him now like a gaoler, uttering threats, potential threats anyway. The time for redemption might be at hand: Mr Bewdley was convinced the bulge in the dressing-gown pocket was caused by a pistol. He gripped the sides of his seat.

He said in a very calm voice, quite unable to suppress the words, 'You married Miss Spender.'

Van Buren started, eyes widening. 'What has my wife to do with you?'

'I trust she's well.'

Van Buren said, 'It seems there's something I don't know. What, precisely, are you saying, Bewdley?'

Mr Bewdley licked at his lips. 'You can't have it all your own way. Privilege . . . it isn't fair. I'm no Socialist, God forbid, but I don't go along with privilege taking all. Miss Spender *and* the bullion. Oh, no!' Very suddenly Mr Bewdley shot from the chair like a bullet. The Dutchman was taken utterly by surprise and, badly winded, fell backwards, doubled in agony. As he crashed to the cabin floor his head impacted hard against the edge of the wash-hand-basin cabinet. Mr Bewdley lost no time; he went for the pocket with the bulge and found he had been correct. There was a pistol, and he brought it out and drew back the hammer.

ii

Directly after the blast of the shot Victoria appeared at the head

136

of the companion ladder and called out to Halfhyde. The gale tore her voice away; her face was a white blur in the darkness: heavy cloud had come up and the moon was obscured.

Halfhyde went across to her. She said, 'He's done it. Bewdley's done it. He's shot van Buren. The bloke's dead.' She was verging on hysteria.

'What's Pieters and –'

'They're in van Buren's cabin and they've got their bloody guns out. I don't want to go back down there, mate –'

'You're not going to. Come with me – and hold tight.'

'What about those blokes?'

He said, 'They'll stay below till the weather moderates. They aren't fools, nor do they want to commit suicide. They'll not interfere on deck while the ship's in danger. Come on.'

He kept an arm around the girl's body and they moved for the ladder to the waist, Halfhyde keeping one hand on the lifeline rigged fore and aft along the deck from poop to fo'c'sle. Victoria had been soaked to the skin the moment she had come clear of the companionway and she was shivering violently. The ship shuddered to the impact of another sea dropping aft, and more green water swirled as Halfhyde clung to the lifeline and the girl. Moving for'ard in a series of checks and rushes, Halfhyde reached the deckhouse containing the petty officers' accommodation.

With difficulty he swung the door open and pushed her inside. 'Stay in there,' he said. 'Don't come out till I send for you, Victoria. Just sit it out – at least you'll be able to dry out and stay dry, so long as we don't spring any seams. And don't worry, we're going to be all right.'

'But that little Bewdley –'

'Don't worry about him either.' Halfhyde shut the door on her and went back aft to the poop. Bewdley's action was now a *fait accompli* and there was nothing to be gained by worrying over it. But Bewdley couldn't have chosen a worse moment, when the whole attention of the master and crew was on the safety of the ship. And he had pre-empted Halfhyde's options now; the clash had caught Halfhyde unready, and from now on

137

it was going to be so much the harder to mount an effective strike-back, at any rate while they were at sea. Victoria had said the guns were out; they would remain out now and there would be no mercy shown. The *Glen Halladale* would run her easting down to the Leeuwin and beyond, with her master a puppet dancing to the bullion stealers' tune. The one card Halfhyde was left with was the fact that without him and enough deckhands to sail the ship, the bandits would never make the land.

Meanwhile those bandits were doing what he had forecast to Victoria: they were keeping their heads down and remaining below. He had time to formulate some kind of plan; but not yet. The ship itself had to come first. She seemed to be taking it; her hull was intact and the carpenter, sounding round below, had reported her watertight. Such a happy state of affairs might not last; seams were going to be sprung aft if the terrible pounding action of the seas was kept up for much longer. There was nothing to be done about that except to keep running before the gale and hope to stand clear of the worst.

iii

Mr Bewdley was in a sorry state. Shortly after he had fired point blank into the Dutchman, and the body had slumped back against him, pouring blood, the man Pieters had appeared with the scar-faced Mahon, both of them flourishing revolvers, heavy ones. They hadn't killed Mr Bewdley but Mahon, pushing past his friend Pieters, had smashed the barrel of his revolver into the little man's mouth, breaking a number of his teeth, splitting his lips and causing massive bruising below the nose. Mr Bewdley had gone down whimpering like a whipped dog, tasting blood each time he swallowed, and in great pain. He believed the shot must have been heard on deck, unless the noise of the gale had drowned it, and he had been expectant of succour from Halfhyde. When none came he decided that Halfhyde must be too occupied on deck and could spare none of his hands from the task of taking off the sails or whatever it might be. That, Mr Bewdley could understand.

'You little bugger,' Mahon said, lifting the heavy revolver again. Pieters grabbed his arm, told him to lay off. Then they were joined by Flannery, limping from some damage caused when Halfhyde had kicked him down the companion ladder. Flannery was in a vicious mood.

'We'd best take over the whole ship,' he said, 'and have done with it.'

Pieters nodded. 'We may have to, but not until the weather improves. In the meantime we have some re-thinking to do. With van Buren gone . . . there's going to be a difference, you'll agree.'

'In what way? We still head for Amsterdam, don't we?'

'I don't know,' Pieters answered. 'I don't know yet. There might be difficulties . . . .' He didn't elaborate.

'Where else, then? Australia?'

Pieters shrugged. 'It's a big place, all right. Big enough to get lost in.'

'I don't know so much,' Flannery said with a touch of unease. 'No place is so big the coppers don't find you in the end, not when you've got a hundred thousand quids' worth of gold bullion round your neck, and bloody staff officers going mad back in South Africa –'

'If they are. Van Buren covered that, remember. There could be ways –'

'You go in,' Flannery said, 'in a square-rigger – enter some port like Melbourne, or maybe Fremantle, and you bugger off into the bush, and no one asks any questions?'

Pieters laughed. 'There's any number of places you can land in Australia without being seen, Flannery – so long as you don't make the approach in anything too big. If you understand me?'

Flannery looked at him. 'Maybe I do, maybe I don't.'

'Then I'll explain. When the weather's suitable – and when we're not far off the Australian coast – that's when we seize the ship. Till then, we play it down, accept the killing of van Buren and carry on as we've been doing so far. Once we've got the ship, we sink her –'

'Sink her, eh. How?'

139

Pieters said, 'I'll find a way, don't you worry. Then we make our getaway in the boat and head for somewhere quiet, going ashore after dark. The *Glen Halladale*, she'll be written off lost at sea. Lost with all hands and the cat. And the gold.'

'But the crew – Halfhyde and the girl, and the –'

Pieters interrupted impatiently. 'Use your brain, Flannery. We're armed, they're not. There won't be anyone left alive. So – until the time's right, I say again, we're docile, but we maintain a watch on the poop –'

'What about Bewdley?'

Pieters hesitated, lifted his head and scratched reflectively beneath his jaw. 'Might be useful,' he said, but didn't explain why. 'You never know your luck. But he'll have to stay where he is, no contact with Halfhyde or any of the ship's crew or the woman. That means he'll have to be watched too.' He stirred at the quivering body with a foot. 'Hear that, did you?'

'Yes,' Mr Bewdley answered in a faint voice.

'Don't give any trouble, then, or you won't last long. I'm not taking any risks once they become unnecessary. I may change my mind about letting you live in any case. So just watch it.'

iv

The wind continued to blow at severe gale force for three more days, during which time Halfhyde scarcely ever left the poop and the hands got little respite and no food beyond cold bully beef issued from the galley by the cook. At the end of the three days everyone was bleary-eyed, staggering from sheer weariness, and two men had fallen from aloft into the rearing seas with no possibility of rescue. The man who had taken the falling yard in his stomach earlier had died. Three men had suffered varying degrees of injury, one with a broken leg, two with arms badly gashed when they had been thrown violently against splintered woodwork. These three were being tended in the saloon by Victoria, though there was little she could do but bathe and bandage them. Working from the text of *The Ship Captain's Medical Guide* she had put a splint on the broken leg and could only pray she had made a reasonable job of it and that the man would not go through life, if he lived at all, with a leg permanently twisted as a result of its having been badly set.

From now on the ship was going to be short-handed, and there was a long haul ahead of them. Halfhyde, pacing the poop again after a couple of hours' sleep following the moderation of the weather, and looking now at a clear blue sky with cloud scudding along before a wind that was no more than fresh, had estimated from the chart and a noon sight with his sextant that they should be off Cape Leeuwin within some twenty days, and that was only the first leg. During the tail end of the storm he had had words with Pieters, firstly about the killing of van Buren and then as to the progress of the voyage.

'I shall be short-handed,' he'd said. 'Too much so for a long voyage and the passage of Cape Horn.'

'What are you asking, Captain? A port of call, to sign your replacements?'

'Yes. That's vital. There are other things as well.'

'Such as?'

Halfhyde gestured aloft. 'I've lost a good deal of canvas, and used up much of my spare suit of sails. If we meet trouble off the Horn, or in the South Atlantic . . . and there is also structural damage, some of it beyond the capacity of the ship to make good as should be done. In my opinion we should make our landfall north of the Leeuwin, and head for the Swan River.'

'Fremantle?'

Halfhyde nodded. 'If you wish to be sure of reaching Amsterdam, we must enter port and accept some delay.'

Pieters appeared to consider the matter, stroking his chin and looking thoughtful. After a while he said, 'Well, I accept your opinion as a seaman, Captain Halfhyde. To that extent we're in your hands, of course. I'll think about it –'

Halfhyde snorted. 'The matter requires no thinking about to a sane man, Pieters. I've given you the facts. You'll have to abide by them.'

'Uh-huh. Well, if that's to be, then there'll have to be safeguards.'

'Yes. I expected that.'

'Your woman, Captain. She'll be held incommunicado all the time till we're away again. Any trouble – I needn't say more, I think. And no one goes ashore.'

Pieters went below then. Soon after, as soon as the weather had allowed, the sailmaker had fitted van Buren and the dead seaman with canvas shrouds and they had been given a sea committal, with Halfhyde reading the words of the service as the bodies slid from a tilted plank into the wide wastes of the Southern Ocean at the world's bottom. Halfhyde had been fended off from all contact with Mr Bewdley: like Victoria if port was made, Pieters said with steel in his voice and his hand on the butt of his revolver, he was held incommunicado.

Now, thinking back to his conversation with Pieters about the Fremantle call, it seemed to Halfhyde that the man had conceded somewhat quickly. He might perhaps have volunteered his bandits to assist the depleted crew, for what they would have been worth; but he had not. With his life at stake, or at least his freedom, he might have insisted on completing the voyage as best possible; but he had not.

It had all been a shade too easy. And there was the fact that Bewdley was being allowed no communication. Bewdley might therefore be considered to have some knowledge that he, Halfhyde, had not.

What was in Pieters' mind? He and his collaborators would face impossible danger in Fremantle or any other port, whether or not Victoria was to be the hostage. They had known that from the start. Berthing pilot, port officials, customs and immigration, health requirements – Australia always produced a swarm of men with sheaves of forms and someone was going to smell the rat of a ship and master under duress, would sense the cracks in the façade. There was something going on in Pieters' mind and it didn't take Halfhyde long to work out what it must be.

THIRTEEN

Pieters and his gang couldn't be everywhere at once: Halfhyde was able to pass the word separately to Edwards and Culver and the bosun under cover of discussions about the repairs and so on. 'The act of piracy is to be finalized,' he said to the first mate, 'an all-out attack. It won't be yet, obviously. They still need us all.'

'But as soon as they don't . . .'

'Exactly, Mr Edwards. That moment'll come once we've made our landfall. Or, if they can find out when we expect to make that landfall, it may come a little earlier.'

'Why's that, sir?'

Halfhyde said, 'Because they may not want to go into action in sight of the land. They won't know who might have us in his telescope. If there's to be fighting and murder, it's best done beyond the horizon.'

'They won't have any means of knowing, sir.'

'No, probably not. But guesses can be fairly accurate, Mr Edwards, the more so when inspired by a look at the chart. Pieters is no fool – yet I believe he can be fooled by a little deviousness on our part.' Halfhyde paused, took a quick look around the deck. 'Each time the noon sight is taken, I wish our position to be shown wrongly on the chart, say, fifty miles short of the true fix. Is that understood?'

'It is, sir,' Edwards answered. 'We shall then –'

'Make our landfall before Pieters is ready. With luck it should give us several days in hand, and one fine morning

Pieters will find himself within sight of the Darling Hills!'

Edwards shook his head. 'I see a snag, sir. What if he reads the patent log?'

Halfhyde frowned: the first mate had a point. The patent log, streamed astern throughout every voyage, gave a record of the day's run, of the distance covered through the water. From this Pieters could form a reasonably accurate estimation of how much farther they had to go, and, assuming he could work out distances on the chart, not a hard thing even for a layman, he could quite quickly bowl out the stratagem of the incorrectly marked daily position. But it might prove impossible to deflect Pieters away from the log without arousing some suspicions in the man's mind.

'The log will be cut adrift, Mr Edwards,' Halfhyde said, 'tonight, after full dark. See to that, if you please.'

'Aye, aye, sir.'

Halfhyde next had words with the bosun. 'Now, Patcham, a lot's going to be up to you. You'll know by now who you can trust among the fo'c'sle crowd, including the men signed in Durban?'

'Aye, sir, I do. There's some doubtful, such as'll likely go with the majority, and there's one or two who'd stick a knife in anyone's back once the word spreads about that there bullion, sir.'

'And the majority?'

Patcham blew out a long breath. 'With us, sir, I believe, though you can never be certain sure when the circumstances are funny like –'

'But you'll know whose loyalty is beyond question. Take them, and only them, into your confidence, Patcham. And then make sure they're in no doubt that any talking out of turn will lead to their own deaths and the deaths of everyone else in the crew. Pieters is playing for high stakes and he'll go the whole hog.'

'What d'you reckon 'e means to do, sir?' Patcham asked.

'Seize the ship, openly – as I said, complete the act of piracy on the high seas. After that – well, we shall have to wait and see.'

'Surely he'll not try to take the ship into a port, sir?'

Halfhyde gave a grim laugh. 'I'd doubt that very strongly! No, he'll enter no port. Not aboard the *Glen Halladale* at all events!'

Patcham looked baffled. 'Not, sir? But –'

'The seaboat, Patcham. Once we're close enough, he can use the seaboat after disposing of all of us. But if my stratagem works he may well be too late. That's what we must hope for – and be ready for his reaction when it comes.'

ii

The days passed in better weather: clear skies with a boisterous wind behind, the endless westerlies along which ships had sailed around the world for centuries past. Wonderful weather for a seaman, the canvas tautly straining from the yards, the ship bowling along with a big bone in her teeth and the wake streaming and tumbling behind in the confusion of the following waves. By Halfhyde's estimate they were now some four days' sailing from Fremantle; the patent log had long since been cut away and the word passed that the line had started to strand after the gale and had not been replaced as it should have been. The spare log was brought up and streamed but Edwards had contrived to damage it, and its message when hauled in was nil sea-miles covered. Pieters had offered no comment; and the ship's daily position as pencilled onto the chart had never been queried. So far, so good. There remained the question of the seaboat. Halfhyde could see no other ploy by Pieters than what he had suggested to the bosun – the use of the seaboat after dealing with all hands in the crew. No one had made the suggestion that the boat should be smashed: to any seaman at sea, that would be tantamount to murder, since lives depended, or might ultimately depend, upon the seaboat. Always at sea, at any moment, disaster could come and the boat was the only salvation, the only hope, if the ship should founder. Even so, Halfhyde was considering it and holding it as a last resort. When the attack came, then would be the time for

145

desperate measures to inhibit Pieters and his schemes.

In the meantime Mr Bewdley was as incommunicado as Pieters had said he would be. Never a sight of him on deck, never a sight of him in the saloon. His meals were taken to him by Pieters himself; and one of the armed men was continually on watch in his cabin. Halfhyde himself spent most of his time on deck, endlessly pacing the poop and uselessly thinking, trying to envisage all the angles, how the attack would materialize, trying to see into the minds of the authorities at the Cape. He expected no pursuit of Pieters; the track of the *Glen Halladale* wouldn't be known. She had ostensibly sailed from Durban for Liverpool; it would be a while yet before she was reported missing. And as it happened, no other ships had been raised along the Roaring Forties, no master with the customary question by flag signal: what ship, and where from, and where bound? Had such a ship been raised within signalling distance, Pieters would have been, of course, ready with false answers so scant hope there would have been of help from that direction . . . .

Victoria was with him for a good deal of the time. Pieters didn't appear to object, but one or other of his men, or he himself, was always at hand on the poop; there was no relaxation of the watch. But Victoria didn't speak about the current problem; there was nothing to be gained by that. She talked instead about the more distant future: she refused resolutely to believe that Pieters was going to get away with the destruction of the ship and crew. She asked what that future might hold for Halfhyde, once they were finished with the jinx of the gold bullion.

He shrugged but went along with her mood of optimism. 'Back to Cape Town,' he said.

'The Cape for orders?'

'Yes. And possibly a court martial. I'm still a lieutenant of the reserve, Victoria.'

'They'll never do that to you! Not after all that's –'

'If I lose the gold finally, they'll do anything their lordships feel fit. And there's still Ladysmith in the balance for all we

146

know.'

'You won't lose the gold,' she said stoutly. 'Let's forget it, mate, eh? Let's forget the court martial, too. We go back to Cape Town, you said. After that, what? Do you wait for another naval appointment, or do you sail back to Liverpool and wait to take over the *Taronga Park* again?'

'It all depends on the naval authorities, Victoria – the Admiralty in London.' Halfhyde paused. 'What about you? Would you feel inclined to stay in Australia, if we land back there again?'

'Would you?' she asked.

'I told you, Victoria, the choice isn't mine in any event. I have to take the ship back to Cape Town.'

'Well,' she said, 'that's my answer too. I'm coming with you, mate, too right I bloody am!'

The urchin face was turned up to him and he fancied he caught the glint of tears. There was the clear look of love; he felt unworthy of it, knew that he could offer her nothing beyond his own companionship and that of the sea, which was his life. Marriage was not possible, as she well knew. There was still Halfhyde's estranged wife, Mildred, in Portsmouth. Would Victoria Penn sail the seas with him, voyage after voyage, year after year until they grew old together, still unwed so long as Mildred lived? There was, of course, divorce: but Mildred would never give him grounds for that.

He said, 'Don't throw yourself away, my dear. You're young, and your life's before you.'

'I said, I'm coming with you.'

iii

After the noon sight had been taken that day, Pieters approached Halfhyde whilst he was entering the ship's position falsely on the chart.

'How far to go, Captain?'

'We should raise the coast in four days' time,' Halfhyde answered.

Pieters nodded. He said no more; he was, Halfhyde believed,

completely unsuspicious as to the incorrect positions shown on the chart. By Halfhyde's estimate the *Glen Halladale* would in fact make her Western Australia landfall by first light in two days' time. By then he would be ready, with the trustworthy hands as detailed by the bosun positioned to the best advantage to deal with sudden attack by the armed men. Pieters would be caught on the hop, unprepared for the sight of the land, and that would give Halfhyde the first advantage. As soon as Pieters had left him, Halfhyde made his way for'ard for a word with his first mate, who was supervising some work on the fo'c'sle head.

'Two days now, Mr Edwards. First light. Pass the word to Patcham, if you please.'

'Aye, aye, sir.'

'Each man to be handy by a belaying-pin. And remember, it'll be a fight to the death if our theorizing's proved correct.'

'Yes, sir. You don't think Pieters may hold his hand, that he'll have a hot reception prepared for us in Fremantle? If the Dutch government's involved, they could have –'

'Highly unlikely! Fremantle's a chance port. We were never intended to enter *any* port, and the fact we're doing so is purely fortuitous. However – if Pieters doesn't attack, then he doesn't, that's all about it, and we shall live to fight another day, as I should much prefer. Once into any port, I'll back myself to stop Pieters in his tracks and he knows it. That's why I'm convinced the trouble will start the moment Pieters sees the land.'

iv

Mr Bewdley had suffered abominably in the close confinement of his cabin. With the guard always present there was no privacy at all; worse than that was the knowledge that he had a duty to perform, a duty to inform Halfhyde as to what Pieters intended, and that he would have no opportunity to do so. This he felt very keenly. It was in his hands and his alone to alert the captain and cut the ground from under the feet of the gunmen. His mind had worked ceaselessly around the problem and had got nowhere. What would Pieters do to sink the ship as he had said he would? Open the sea-cocks, lay about with axes to cut down the masts and sails – start a fire? Yes – a fire!

Almost certainly, Bewdley felt, it would be that. It would be the obvious way, the most surely effective. Mr Bewdley was no seaman but he believed it possible that a ship with the sea-cocks opened might sink only to the waterline, and thereafter, or anyway for a very long time, lie waterlogged and drifting, to be urged by the prevailing westerlies and the ocean currents closer and closer to Australia to become a threat to Pieters when he believed himself safe. No – fire would be the answer, a burning of the ship right through her timbers, down through the holds to gut the vessel and leave nothing but a shell that would quickly fill and sink. All the crew dead, himself dead as well, and Pieters and his gang away in the boat with the bullion.

He had to do something, but what?

Mr Bewdley, as the dreadful days passed, grew desperate. He thought about a sudden shout, a yell that might carry through the cabin door and along the alleyway to reach Halfhyde's ears, perhaps on the poop, perhaps in his cabin, or indeed the ears of the woman or of any member of the crew. But what could a single yell convey – the single yell that would be all he was permitted before his guard stifled him, perhaps for ever? It would, of course, convey nothing except that he had reached the end of his tether. So he decided not to shout. And a hammering on the bulkhead would produce no better result.

Mr Bewdley sat motionless but for the shake in his limbs. He felt as though he was approaching madness, that he might go berserk, or that his head would burst asunder with the sense of claustrophobia and frustration that was building up inside it. In the end he would die, and his name would be execrated in Cape Town as the man who had allowed the bullion to be stolen and the course of the war to be altered against his own side. Mr Bewdley was well enough aware of the intrigues and innuendoes of governmental life and he would not put it past belief that gossip would say, after he was dead, that he had aided and abetted the evildoers for what he believed he might get out of it. Even Mr Bewdley had his enemies in the ingrown world of the secretariat . . . .

It was fortunate that his poor old dad had gone too, though in all conscience he could scarcely have lived this long in any case. He would have been much grieved by the scandal.

Mr Bewdley suddenly recalled that he had recently killed Miss Spender's husband. She was now a widow, not of himself but of van Buren. He gave a laugh, a hysterical one. If any of them came through this, which was unlikely, then Miss Spender was in for scandal not brought about by himself. The widow of van Buren would be no better off than the widow of Bewdley, for what that was worth. He laughed again, and went on laughing.

'Shut up,' Mahon said. When Mr Bewdley went on laughing, Mahon got up, his scarred face vicious, and slapped Mr Bewdley hard on each cheek, but failed to stop the crazy noise. Tears were now running down Mr Bewdley's face and his cheeks stung. Mahon was wearing a ring, a heavy one, which had brought lacerations and blood. Mr Bewdley's head buzzed, his mind seemed to lift and fly away, and he continued laughing and crying, and he couldn't get his act of killing – it could possibly be called murder – out of his brain. It gnawed like a rat . . . a rat in a sinking ship, gnawing its way out to a watery death. A man, or a rat, who had killed once could kill again. That was why they hanged murderers, of course . . . .

Mahon was looking at Bewdley, looking at him dangerously. If he could somehow get hold of Mahon's revolver, and shoot Mahon like he had shot van Buren, then there would at least be one man less for Halfhyde to deal with when the attack was mounted, one less gun to fire upon unarmed seamen. Mr Bewdley stopped laughing suddenly; he knew he would never to able to wrest the revolver from Mahon, he wouldn't have the strength, and one couldn't really expect to repeat what had been done before. Mahon would be ready for that. With the hysterical laughter stopped, Mahon relaxed but remained watchful. The day was going now, and soon it was dark. Mahon got to his feet, struck a match and lit the hanging lamp.

It smoked badly, and Mahon carefully trimmed the wick down. In so doing, his attention was momentarily drawn away from Mr Bewdley. Bewdley took what he saw as perhaps his only chance to assist Halfhyde.

He reached out a hand stealthily. His mind was very confused but if he could get the revolver out of the holster he was going to shoot Mahon.

He was scarcely breathing now.

The hand had almost touched the butt of the revolver when Mahon became aware of what was happening. He swung round, brought his fist down hard on Bewdley's wrist, knocking it away. Bewdley gave a short yelp of pain, then saw Mahon draw a clasp-knife from his pocket, and flick it open. Terrified now, Mr Bewdley reacted instinctively. He hit out wildly in an attempt to keep the man away, keep out of range of the knife. A lucky swing of his fist, by accident rather than design, took Mahon on the point of the chin. Mahon jerked his head backwards and hit against the swinging lamp, hard. It came free of its mounting and crashed down to the cabin floor. Paraffin flew, ignited, spraying over the woodwork and the bunk sheets. Mahon lunged with the knife, a vicious downward cut into Bewdley's stomach, and Bewdley screamed.

v

The scream ripped through the night's darkness, reaching Halfhyde on the poop. He ran for the companion. The man with the gun, the man on watch – one of those who had driven the covered wagon up from Cape Town – got there before him.

'Stand back or I'll shoot.'

Halfhyde faced him squarely. 'Shoot, then. You'll not be thanked by your friend Pieters.'

He pushed past and the man didn't interfere. As he stepped onto the ladder the smell of burning came up from below. He went down at the rush, found the saloon alleyway filling with smoke. Pieters was there with Flannery and Mahon, and the second mate, Culver, assisted by the steward, was busy with the fire buckets in the cabin occupied by Bewdley.

Halfhyde pushed through. Bewdley was lying on the floor of the cabin, blood welling from his stomach. Halfhyde bent and dragged him clear, out into the alleyway. The little man was in a bad way but living yet. He mumbled something incoherent – something about wishing only to give a warning. Halfhyde made a quick examination: it was doubtful if he was going to last.

Looking up, Halfhyde found Victoria at his side. He said, 'Stay by him. I'll get him into the saloon.' He lifted Bewdley and carried him from the alleyway, laying him on the settee.

The smoke was increasing; as Halfhyde ran back into the alleyway he found the wash-deck hoses being run out from the pumps, through the for'ard door from the waist, and Patcham directing the water into the burning cabin. The space was well alight by this time and the smoke was thick and billowing; the fire had managed to get a good hold. And a moment later there was a shout down the companionway from the poop.

'Captain, sir! Fire's broken through the deckhead!'

Halfhyde went up the ladder fast. On the port side of the poop there was a red glow in the deck planking, already charring, and flames, fanned high by the following wind, were licking upwards at the bulwarks and the cordage of the standing rigging. Edwards was calling for hands to lay aft with more of the wash-deck hoses, while, at the same time, doing what he could to try to douse the flames with sand from the fire buckets aft of the wheel. Halfhyde joined him; but the fire was gaining with every second, responding to the wind's breath, and already there was a lick of flame running along the bolt-ropes of the spanker as it strained from the boom. It would not be long now before the canvas caught. Halfhyde passed the order for the spanker to be let go before this could happen and spread the fire to all the rest of the canvas.

Pieters had come up from the saloon alleyway. He ran across to Halfhyde. 'Can't you get it under control, for God's sake, Captain?'

'That's what I'm trying to do.'

Pieters wiped sweat from his face. 'What are the chances?'

'Poor, I fancy. Fire at sea soon gets a grip. I may have to abandon, but we shall see.'

The Dutchman's voice was edgy. 'Taking it calmly, aren't you?'

'Would you have me give way to panic?'

Pieters scowled. 'What about the gold?'

'To hell with the gold,' Halfhyde answered crisply. 'I'll be glad enough to see it melt!' He added, 'The best thing you and your bandits can do now is work with the hands to save the ship – and your own lives into the bargain.'

Pieters stared at him for a moment, his face working with many emotions – fear, anger, greed were all there in his eyes. He muttered something that Halfhyde failed to catch, then turned away, leaving the poop by the starboard ladder running down to the waist. Halfhyde's attention was on his ship; he put Pieters from his mind. All the hoses were in action, and Patcham was now leading the hands in an attempt to cut away the burning rigging and prevent the lick of flame from reaching any more of the canvas. By this time the spanker had been taken down and its burning doused as it lay encumbering the poop with its massive folds. The decking of the poop itself was growing hot and the charring had spread. Water hissed and bubbled, turning to steam. All aboard were now on deck; the after accommodation had been evacuated; two of the fo'c'sle hands were still directing a hose through the entry from the waist, two more were sending water down the companion from the poop, but the stream from the hand pump in the waist was thin and seemed to be having little effect. The whole of the after part of the ship was in the full grip of the fire, and heavy black smoke swept out blindingly. Mr Bewdley had been carried from the saloon, and lay in the scuppers to starboard, his life blood draining away.

Halfhyde roared out, 'The seaboat, Mr Edwards! Have a care for the seaboat. Put a hose on her and keep it there!'

'Aye, aye, sir.' The first mate ran down into the waist himself and saw to the order. Coming back to the poop he joined Halfhyde. He said, 'I think we should get the seaboat away before the fire spreads further, sir.' He added, 'There's the question of the gold, sir.'

'Yes, I'm well aware of that, Mr Edwards.'

Halfhyde looked astern, at the wind and sea. The gale-force conditions of most of the passage had fallen away considerably, and although there was more than enough wind to fan the flames and increase the danger Halfhyde anticipated no undue difficulty in getting the seaboat into the water safely and he believed that the time to abandon was in fact approaching fast; but there was the gold and it couldn't be ignored in spite of what he had said to Pieters. He still had a responsibility for it and its return to Cape Town or Durban and perhaps, if it was not already too late, its safe delivery to General Buller's camp on the Tugela. And there was Bewdley, very much upon his conscience. Bewdley had behaved bravely throughout and, whether he lived or died, to jettison the gold would be a poor recompense for duty done.

Halfhyde said, 'The gold will be brought up, Mr Edwards.'

'The hands –'

'Fully employed – yes. Well, it'll not be brought up by the hands, Mr Edwards. Pieters went down to the tween deck some few minutes ago, as I observed – and I doubt if he's gone below for his health at a time of danger!'

'You think he'll load the bullion aboard the seaboat, sir?'

Halfhyde nodded. 'I'm sure of it. And the operation's to be closely watched. Have you heard any whispers among the fo'c'sle hands, Mr Edwards, about the gold?'

'No, sir –'

'No more have I. But the secrecy'll not survive the loading into the boat. There may be trouble, and we must be ready for it when it comes.'

The first mate nodded. Undoubtedly there could be manifestations of greed, even in the current danger. Seamen were always ready to try their luck and were seldom deterred by considerations of risk and danger; every ship had its element of unsavoury characters, villains, men with more than an eye to the main chance, and many emotions could be released when they saw riches for the taking – for the taking by force, by the use of the belaying-pin or the gun against the afterguard and their own messmates from the fo'c'sle. The tougher ones would win out; the seaboat would be got away with the gold and the *Glen Halladale* would be left to burn to the waterline, and then to sink with the charred remains of those who had been held away from the departing boat.

vi

'Right,' Pieters said with satisfaction.

The bullion had been stowed in the tween deck, which was carrying no other cargo; the *Glen Halladale* had been officially bound home in ballast and the leather bags, said to be holding the personal possessions of the Dutchman and his accomplices, were securely padlocked to the iron stanchions along the tween deck. These bags had now been carried for'ard to the tween deck hatch and, by a combination of pushing from below and pulley-hauley from above, had been brought up the companion to lie on deck ready to be hefted into the seaboat, now freed of its chocks and ready on the falls to be swung out over the rushing water. 'Get it aboard now,' Pieters ordered, and made ready to lend a hand himself. He glanced aft towards the poop: he saw Halfhyde with the first mate, moving now down the starboard ladder to the waist, coming out of the thick swirls of smoke and the licking tongues of flame.

'Can't be long now,' Pieters said. Already some of the hands, the less reliable ones – those signed on in Durban were among them – were placing themselves handy for the seaboat, anticipating the order to abandon ship. By now Pieters had his revolver out, openly. He used this to co-opt four of the seamen to the task of heaving the bags aboard. The sheer weight took them by surprise: there was more in those leather bags than clothing, and whatever it was, it had to be of value. And the captain . . . he wasn't making any move to interfere with the loading of the extra weight, so the bags must be of value to more persons than their apparent owners. That might be worth bearing in mind.

By now the very air seemed to be filled with flying sparks and the terrible crackle of burning woodwork as the wind chased

155

the flames along the masts and yards. Halfhyde's voice was heard: 'Mr Edwards! Patcham! Pass the word . . . all hands, abandon ship!'

As the cry went along the decks, Halfhyde was seen to vanish into the smoke, but not for long. He reappeared with Victoria and the steward, assisting the latter to carry Mr Bewdley to the seaboat. Bewdley was alive yet, it seemed, white-faced and bloodstained. Halfhyde passed the final orders.

'Mr Edwards, stand by to see Mr Bewdley and Miss Penn safely into the seaboat.'

'Aye, aye, sir.'

'Patcham?'

'Here, sir!'

'As soon as Mr Bewdley and Miss Penn are embarked, the boat's to be swung out but not lowered until I give the order. The hands will jump across from the bulwarks, and the lowerers will be the last down the falls before the order's passed to slip.'

'Yes, sir.' Patcham turned away, calling for hands to stand by at the davits. There was shouting and confusion now, the gold temporarily forgotten in the interest of self-preservation. There were some men who preferred to be standing ready to embark quickly themselves rather than tend the falls and perhaps be left behind should a sudden sea take the boat in its grip and force it to be slipped early, and these were hanging back from involvement. Patcham dealt with them peremptorily, a belaying-pin in his fist as he enforced the orders, his weather-beaten face streaming sweat in the increasing heat.

Taking a last look around his decks, feeling a surge of hatred for Pieters and his gunmen, Halfhyde said, 'All right, Mr Edwards. Get Mr Bewdley aboard and see him settled as comfortably as possible.'

Edwards jumped up onto the battened-down cover of the after hatch, where he was on a level with the seaboat's gunwale. As he bent to take Bewdley's feet and start to lift the inert body with the steward's assistance, there was a harsh word from the Dutchman.

'Stay where you are! And you, Captain.'

Halfhyde's fists clenched. 'Damn you to hell, Pieters! You'll not impede operations now. My orders are to be obeyed, not yours.'

Pieters had his revolver aimed at Victoria. Halfhyde saw that all the bandits had their guns out: Flannery, Mahon, the two wagon drivers . . . and already they were swinging themselves up to board the seaboat and fend off anyone else who tried to embark. Halfhyde was about to jump towards Victoria and put himself between her and the line of fire from Pieters when he saw a cautious movement from Patcham. The bosun, standing by the after davit, belaying-pin in hand, was moving closer to Pieters. But as he lifted the belaying-pin to bring it down on the Dutchman's head he was seen by Flannery.

Flannery shouted a warning, and Pieters swung round sharply. Patcham brought the belaying-pin down with smashing force but missed and overbalanced, lurching forward. Pieters' revolver flamed and the bullet took the bosun in the chest, straightening his body with a jerk and sending it backwards to lie sprawled on the deck.

FOURTEEN

'Now it's my orders that are going to be obeyed,' Pieters said. 'Everyone stand back, away from the boat. Anyone who doesn't, they go the same way as the bosun, and that's a promise.'

His gun in his hand, he backed towards the boat. Flannery and the others went with him, a compact and determined group.

As they went aboard Pieters said, 'Four men, four seamen. That's all I'm taking – four men who'll lower us into the water and then come down and man the oars. And don't all rush at once or you'll all die. Understood?'

The men Halfhyde had already identified as the bad element moved towards the davits; most of the good men hung back. They would not leave the ship unless all hands went with them. They couldn't be all that far off the Australian coast by now, and they might have a fighting chance if the life-jackets kept them afloat for long enough; there might yet be timber to be got from the *Glen Halladale* before she succumbed, and a raft might be made. It was a slim enough hope, but it was better than Pieters and the guns.

The seaboat was swung out quickly and was lowered on the falls until it took the water with a slapping sound, and was surged for'ard by the waves.

That was when Halfhyde moved.

As the lowerers swarmed down the falls to the boat, two for'ard and two aft, and then stood by to cast off the blocks,

Halfhyde jumped onto the bulwarks, a belaying-pin in his hand. With all his strength he hurled the heavy, iron pin towards the men at the for'ard end of the seaboat. His aim was good: the belaying-pin took one man in the neck and he went down screaming; the other man lost his balance and went overboard. By this time the after fall had been cast off and, held by the for'ard fall, the boat was taken by the sea's following action and surged out and away from the ship's side, when the waves threw it back like a tethered dog until it impacted against the hull some feet ahead of where it had lain previously.

Halfhyde scrambled down from the bulwarks and shouted for some hands to back up the for'ard fall; Edwards, realizing what he intended to do, led the men himself and threw his weight onto the fall, heaving in over the davit-head, shortening the length and, in effect, binding the great hook fast to the eye in the boat and holding it to the fall so tightly that it would be impossible to cast off.

Yells of anger and fear came up. Then bullets. Pieters and the others were firing indiscriminately and uselessly: the angle of aim was not in their favour, and the men aboard the burning ship were given protection by the bulwarks. Halfhyde kept up the shortening of the remaining fall until the seaboat had been drawn right in to the ship's side and the bow was beginning to come clear of the water. Then he called down to Pieters.

'You'll stay alongside, Pieters, you and the rest. You'll burn with my ship, like the scum you are. But I'm giving you a chance. Throw your revolvers overboard, all of them. Then the rest of us will join you, and the boat will be cast off. In the meantime, any man who tries to cut the falls away will get the same treatment as the man who got the belaying-pin in his neck.'

A stream of abuse, and more bullets, came back, one of them nicking Halfhyde's arm as he dodged down in the lee of the bulwarks. There was little time left now; the whole of the poop was ablaze and it wasn't going to be long before the mizzenmast came down, a flaming, charred wreck with its burning yards and the remains of the rigging and canvas. The fire was stretching out to the main and foremast as well. Already the waist was hot underfoot as the fire spread along the tween deck from the floors of the after accommodation, and twists of smoke were coming up in places, while thicker smoke was starting to come through from the booby hatch. Halfhyde knew that before long his threat to anyone cutting away the holding ropes in the boat would become a somewhat empty one: Pieters would be seeing to it that the seamen's knives were put to good use.

'We shall have to attack in force, Mr Edwards,' he said. 'There's nothing else for it – and no more delay. We must risk the guns now.'

'Miss Penn –'

'Yes. You'll remain aboard with her and Bewdley until I've taken the seaboat. Muster the hands at the bulwarks, if you please.'

'Aye, aye, sir!'

Face blackened with the smoke, Edwards called for the hands to muster by the for'ard davit, keeping low behind the bulwarks. Halfhyde spoke to them briefly, giving his orders. He would himself jump down into the bows of the boat from the bulwarks and the men were to follow hard on his heels, jumping along the whole length and falling on Pieters and the gunmen.

He said, 'The for'ard fall and the sea's action itself will hold the boat close along our side. I know you'll all do your best and not hang back. Are you ready?'

There were nods from the men. They were a tough bunch for the most part, hard men who had lived hard lives. There would be nothing to be gained by hanging back. Moving fast, Halfhyde heaved himself onto the bulwarks above the boat, and jumped.

ii

It was over quickly: the guns had opened and three men had been hit, two of them going over the gunwale into the water and drifting away out of reach, heads down in the sea. But the sheer weight of numbers as the men dropped on them had over-

160

whelmed the bandits and they were soon lying on the bottom boards under the bare fists of the fo'c'sle hands. Edwards, still aboard the *Glen Halladale* as ordered, had sent down a heaving line which Halfhyde had secured in the after end of the seaboat, while the for'ard fall was slacked away so that the boat, held fast fore and aft now, rode on an even keel. Bewdley, wrapped in a length of canvas, was lowered as gently as possible: and then Victoria, tended by Edwards, climbed down the fall to safety. Last of all, Edwards came down; the final links with the *Glen Halladale* were cast off and the boat was propelled away from the ship with the boat-hooks and bearing-out spars.

Only minutes after they had pulled clear under the oars the mainmast went, crashing in a shower of sparks and tongues of flame that licked along the yards and turned the remaining rigging into a tracery of red fire. Halfhyde watched, his very heart-strings wrenched at the sight of a great ship's dying. He felt Victoria's arms go round him.

'Sorry, mate,' she said. 'I'm bloody sorry . . . .'

Her voice was breaking and looking at her he saw the tears. She had taken in something of a shipmaster's love for his ship, something of the sense of personal loss that must accompany any sinking or destruction. That, and a sense of failure.

Victoria said, 'You've saved the bloody gold. That's something, isn't it?'

'And lost a number of lives in the saving. It was never worth that.'

'Maybe not. But you've got Pieters. You've done your duty, I reckon.'

Halfhyde made no response; he was looking back at the blazing ship, which would remain a while, a beacon of sadness to stretch its light across the seas as they pulled away towards the Australian coast. Halfhyde could visualize the collapsing decks, the showers of sparks and blazing planking, the downward crash of the foremast and all the remaining top hamper. He looked for a long while, as if to tear his eyes away would be the final abandonment and a kind of betrayal. The seamen pulled on, making fair progress, with Edwards steering a course for Fremantle by use of the boat's compass. After a while the eastward horizon changed, became sharper, more defined. Halfhyde called the first mate's attention to it.

'Do you see what I see, Mr Edwards?'

'I fancy I do, sir. Land!'

Halfhyde nodded. 'The Darling Hills. We were rather closer in than I'd estimated. You'll realize the likely significance of that, I don't doubt!'

'The ship –'

'Exactly. The blaze'll have been seen from somewhere high up in the hills and reported. Help will be sent. Pieters wouldn't have got away with it in any case – the *Glen Halladale* herself would have seen to that!'

The men at the oars pulled on, given fresh heart and endurance by the knowledge that they had the land in sight, that they were no longer castaways on an endless sea. Within the next two hours Halfhyde's prognostications were proved correct: two steam tugs were sighted ahead, coming along fast from the port of Fremantle with big bones in their teeth as they butted into the westerlies. A cheer went up from the seaboat and was borne away along the wind. One of the tugs continued on a westerly course towards the remains of the *Glen Halladale*, and the other altered for the seaboat with its band of survivors.

The tug's master called across through a megaphone.

'What ship?'

Halfhyde answered. 'The sailing ship *Glen Halladale*, out of Durban. It's a long story. If you'll take us aboard . . . us and some cargo . . . I'll satisfy your curiosity.' Halfhyde looked down at the leather bags containing the bullion: it had caused enough problems and its handing over to the authorities for shipment back to South Africa would be a glad moment. 'By the way . . . what's the news of the war, Captain?'

'Buller's moved at bloody last,' the tugmaster called back. 'Came in on the telegraph cable. He's relieved Ladysmith, just a few days ago – 28 February. All right? Stand by for a heaving line, Captain.'

The tug closed and a line was sent snaking across at the end of a monkey's-fist. Edwards caught it and made it fast in the fore end of the seaboat. Pieters and his confederates glowered in silence: murder had been done, and treason. A heavier rope would await them now. Halfhyde called a warning to the tug that he had prisoners aboard and that although they had been disarmed care should be taken until they were handed over to the authorities in Fremantle. Also he had a seriously wounded man aboard, a civilian from the secretariat in Cape Town, who should be attended by a doctor as soon as possible. As he said this, he looked down at Mr Bewdley. There was some colour now in the little man's cheeks as though good news had wrought a miracle, and he was smiling; perhaps there was hope after all.

Bewdley spoke then. 'Excellent news, Lieutenant Halfhyde. General Buller . . . he attacked notwithstanding, and with success it seems. I think there is vindication for us all in that, don't you agree?'

Halfhyde wasn't so sure; but he nodded and repeated Victoria's words as uttered to himself earlier. 'You've done your duty, Mr Bewdley. The Cape government will be proud of you.'